EASTON

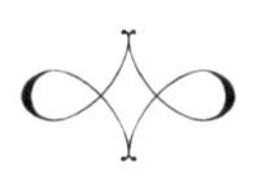

Mandy,
Thank you for reading!
♡ K Webster

K WEBSTER

Easton

Time Served

ISBN-13:978-1548869908

ISBN-10:154886990

Cover Design: All By Design

Photo: Adobe Stock

Editor for Easton: ellie at Love N. Books

Editor for Time Served: PREMA Editing

Formatting: Champagne Formats

A note to the reader…

Easton is a steamy, ***insta-love novella*** sure to make your heart swell. I've also included a small bonus story at the back about another couple called *Time Served*. Make sure you read about them too! I hope you're enjoying these characters in this naughty little town. I've written many more that will be publishing this year, so keep your eyes peeled for those. *Bad Bad Bad* is available now where you'll get your first look at the characters in this town. Plenty more hotness is coming your way! As always, thank you for reading my stories!

Also…this book was formerly known as *Preach*. It was taken down by the Zon because of content. I've made some changes to accommodate them but rest assured that it doesn't take away from the original story. If you read that other book, you won't need to read this one. Thank you for supporting me!

K Webster

A man who made countless mistakes.
A woman with a messy past.

He's tasked with helping her find her way.
She's lost in grief and self-doubt.

Together they begin something innocent…
Until it's not.

His freedom is at risk.
Her heart won't survive another break.

All rational thinking says they
should stay away from each other.
But neither are very good
at following the rules.

A deep, dark craving.
An overwhelming need.
A burn much hotter than any hell
they could ever be condemned to.

He'll give up everything for her…
because without her, he is nothing.

DEDICATION

Matt, I love you, honey.

The hunger for love is much more difficult to remove than the hunger for bread.

Mother Teresa

WARNING:

Easton is a story about a preacher man and a troubled young woman. There is an age gap that some may not like. Additionally, there are some scenes that happen within a church that you may not feel comfortable with. I do make one request. If you offend easily or have any triggers with unconventional relationships or age gaps or religion, please don't read this story. It is an insta-love novella all the way. This story isn't for everyone. However, if you stick with it, I believe you'll truly enjoy the love story I've written for you.

ONE

EASTON

"This is the start of a very bad joke," Dane says with a laugh as he holds open the door to the bar. "A preacher, a judge, and a gay man walk into a bar…"

I snort at my friend I've known since we grew up in the same neighborhood. "Very bad joke. So bad, don't even tell it."

Max, the judge of our stupid joke, laughs as he saunters in and heads straight for our favorite table. "Oh, and look, our joke just got even more lame." He waves at our friend Rick. "Sheriff. Good seeing you here."

Dane chuckles as he makes his way to the bar to order our drinks. Rick strolls over to us with his friend Brandt and shakes our hands.

"I thought you were still in jail," Rick jokes.

"Ha. Ha," I grunt.

"Seriously though," Rick says with a wicked grin. "Won't God strike you dead or some shit for bar hopping?"

"Jesus did love his wine," I argue.

Dane shows back up and hands me a bottle of Bud. "Our boy Easton here is allowed to leave the stuffy confines of that church every now and again for a boys' night. Sheriff, you're just lucky God didn't strike you down for boning a teenager."

Brandt smirks and Rick jabs him with his elbow.

"And you're lucky God didn't strike you down for looking at my ass," Rick retorts to Dane.

"You losers do realize God doesn't strike people down, right?" I laugh before I take a sip of my beer. "He just waits until you die to send you to hell where you'll burn in intense agony for all of eternity."

Max starts laughing along with Brandt while Rick flips me off.

"Way to be a fucking buzzkill, man," Dane grumbles.

EASTON

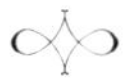

"Your ten o'clock is already here," Lucinda, Brown's Church of Christ's secretary, chirps as I saunter past her. The woman is older than my mom but much more chatty. She's a nice lady though and cares for this church as though it's her own. We have that in common for sure. "She went to the restroom but will be back soon. Shall I send her in?"

My head is throbbing and I could go for a bacon cheeseburger right about now. Going out with Dane and the boys was a lame idea knowing full well I had an appointment this morning.

"Please," I grunt as I walk into my office with my motorcycle helmet under my arm. "Send her in. Can you bring me some coffee when you get a minute? Also, whatever you want, Lucinda, and it's yours. I owe you." I toss the helmet on my desk with a loud thud and fall into my squeaky leather desk chair.

The heavyset woman with greying brown hair shuffles into my office with a wide smile and steaming cup in her grip. "You always look a little worse for the wear on Saturdays," she says in a conspiratorial tone. "I knew you'd be needing this. But I might take you up on that offer later."

I smile gratefully at her as she sets it down on my desk beside my Bible. The same Bible that got me through some tough times when I was incarcerated. It was the one my dad brought to me not long after I went to prison. Finding a job after all the crap I went through was nearly impossible. If it weren't for my father, a deacon at this church, I'd probably still be living at my parents' house trying to sort out my life. Luckily, the church believed in forgiveness and wanted to give me a shot. That was ten years ago, and I've been happy ever since. Had you asked me when I was eighteen what I wanted to be when I grew up, I'd have said a mechanic or something. Not a damn preacher.

But here I am.

And truth be told, I love it.

At first, it was rocky getting people to trust me but I kept at it. With my dad's encouragement and guidance, I powered through the hard times. It's truly been a blessing and I feel as though I'm helping people. And that's always been my goal.

My thoughts drift to the moment things in my life began to change for the better.

"A week in the hole ain't bad, runt," a gruff voice grunts nearby.

My hackles raise and I fist my hands, ready to battle. Last week, three thugs tried to do the unthinkable to me. I was naked and showering when they rushed me. All I could imagine was how horrifying it would be to get raped by three grown ass men. It's something my fucking friends and I would joke about all the time about people in prison. 'Don't get ass raped.' But there I was in fucking prison trying not to get my ass torn out by a trio of black motherfuckers. Rage, like I'd never known before, reared its ugly head. When the shank poked into my thigh and the first prick pressed his hard cock against me, I went mental. Woke up with two swollen shut eyes, bruises all over the fucking place, and a broken rib. Yet my ass was intact.

Black.

That was my mental state.

Black. Black. Black.

Instinct took over and my mind shut down.

The warden and the officers interrogated me on what happened, but I couldn't remember a goddamned thing. All I could remember was the guy on me and then black. That's what I told them too. They weren't too fucking impressed with my answer.

Promised all kinds of shit that pissed me off, including an extended sentence. I'm still waiting to hear back on that one.

"Runt," the voice says again. "I'm talkin' to you."

My left eye is still swollen so I can barely see out of it. I turn to put a face to the voice and wince when I'm staring at nearly seven feet of solid brown muscle. The dude is intimidating as fuck. Tattoos all over his dark flesh making him seem darker. He even has tatts on his face. Who the fuck gets tattoos on their face? I've got one on my back because I thought I was a badass and knew it would piss off my religious parents. Dad was disappointed that I'd ruined my 'temple' with a skull and flames. Mom threw her phone at me. But this guy has them everywhere.

"A week too long," I grumble back at him.

"Speak up, boy, when you're talking to your elders."

His tone reminds me of my dad and it pisses me off.

"Go to hell, asshole," I grind out, my voice a near bellow. "Did you hear that, old man?"

He shakes his head and thumps me in the head. I fist my hands but keep from pummeling him because the hole was a nightmare and I'm not looking to go back anytime soon.

"I'm not going to hell. Christ died upon that cross so that my sins could be absolved," he tells me simply. "I'm saved by the blood of Jesus. Question is, where're you going, runt?"

Oh fuck me.

As if my life hasn't been eighteen years of living in the shadows of my Bible thumpin' parents.

"Apparently I'm going nowhere for the next ten years or so," I snap. "And your Bible shit won't work with me. I know all about Jesus. Mr. Perfect. Just like my fucking dad."

The black guy snorts and thumps me in the head again. "You're an angry little shit, aren't ya?"

"You can't say shit, Bible man. Jesus will condemn you to hell," I mock with a smirk.

He studies me with narrowed eyes. "You read that in The Bible?"

"Thou shall not use thy Lord's name in vain," I say in my best preacher voice.

"You really are stupid, runt. I've got a lot to teach you. Keep you outta trouble 'round here. Nobody messes with a friend of Tom Cat. Question is, are you gonna be a friend to ol' Tom Cat?"

I clench my jaw. "Usually friendships around

here come with stipulations. I'm nobody's bitch, old man. What kind of name is Tom Cat anyway?"

"My name," he mutters. "Thomas Catalina. And I don't think my ma would like it if I got myself a little boyfriend."

I'm not little.

I stand well over six feet and am filled out from playing football in high school. He's just a motherfucking giant.

"What do you want in return?" Everyone wants something in return.

"I want you to listen to what I have to say."

I laugh and shrug. "So tell me."

"Not just now. Every day. I'm going to help you work through that darkness you struggle with," he tells me simply.

"I don't struggle with—"

He thumps me in the forehead again. Fucker is going to give me a bruise.

"Stop fucking thumping me," I roar, causing a few bystanders to cast amused glances our way.

Asshole thumps me again. "You ain't gonna do shit about it, runt. Now get your ass a Bible and get back over here. Class is in session beginning now."

Who needs hell when you're stuck in prison with

a seven-foot Bible thumper dead set on helping you get your gigantic chip off your shoulder?

"Whatever, man," I grumble as I start away from him.

This time, he thumps me in the back of the head. "It wasn't a request, boy. Get your shit. You have two minutes."

Ten minutes later and we're sitting across from each other in the middle of the rec room with our Bibles open. It's every bit as awkward and irritating as it's been the past two years when my dad has tried to help me. For two years, I've been drifting further from my family and reality.

"Who'd you lose?" Tom questions as he puts on some black-rimmed reading glasses. He opens his Bible and thumbs through it. When I don't answer, his dark brown eyes lift to mine. "Real men speak when they're spoken to. Are you a real man?"

I grit my teeth. "Whatever you're doing isn't going to work. My dad already tried."

Tom shrugs. "I'm not doing anything. I'm simply going to read some verses and shoot the breeze with my friend. Friends talk to each other, runt."

As much as it pains me to admit it, I am lonely as fuck. The very idea of having a friend in here—albeit a persistent one—sure beats the alternative. With a sigh, I tell him what he's so clearly dying to hear.

"My older brother died two years ago when I was just sixteen. He was eighteen and had a future ahead of him. When I found his blue body on his bathroom floor, his cheek in a puddle of vomit, it gutted me. He'd overdosed on pain pills that weren't even prescribed to him. They weren't able to revive him and he died that day." My throat is hoarse with emotion but I swallow it down. I refuse to cry in front of him or any of the other inmates around here. "I was happy before then. Normal, like any other teenager. But then, I got angry."

He gives me a nod of his head to proceed.

"It was Dad's fault. He was too hard on him. Nothing was ever good enough. I was the golden child and Elias was the troubled one. I guess…I guess I…"

"Gave your pops hell to punish him?" he quips.

I shrug. "Something like that. I drifted from my parents—especially Dad—and then spun further out of control. Wrong crowds. That sorta shit."

"Have you ever just talked to your pops about his take? I've got three boys of my own. Before I got locked up fourteen years ago, I wasn't good at talking to my kids. Jamal, my middle boy, got involved with the Crips. It wasn't until I got a call from the police at

work one day that I was told just how involved my boy was. They cut my boy's throat." His gaze hardens for a moment but then he gently unfolds a creased page in his Bible. "I wish I'd have been there for him and talked about why he was drifting. Their momma left us not long after the youngest was born. It was just my ma and I raising those boys."

"How'd you end up here?" It's probably rude to ask but he's a prying bastard too.

"Murder."

I gape at him. "For how long you in?"

His nostrils flare. "Life, runt. I'm in here for life."

My blood runs cold in my veins. "Who'd you kill?"

"I found out which gangster killed Jamal and I returned the favor. When his friend tried to stop me, I stabbed him. There was a third gang member that tried to shoot me. Kid couldn't have been older than fifteen..." His eyes soften and he swallows. "I killed him too."

I hear people talking about moments in their lives that spark a change. I'd thought it was bullshit. But right here, right now, talking to this badass motherfucker in for murdering three people who were involved in his son's death, I realize maybe people have bigger problems out there than mine. It also makes me yearn to talk to my dad. Would he have wanted vengeance if someone had murdered one of his boys?

I think about my dad's hard scowls he always wears. I used to think he was fierce when I was a kid. I'm pretty sure had someone else hurt Elias and not Elias, Dad would have gone crazy.

And that puts a smile on my face.

"Easton," Lucinda chirps, waving her hand in front of me in a nervous manner.

I blink away my daze. "What's up?"

"You don't have any more appointments after this one," Lucinda says, her bright smile falling. Her brown eyes drop to her hands that she now wrings together. "I was wondering. You see, I…"

I lift a brow. "Do you need to leave early?"

Her eyes dart to mine and her wrinkled cheeks turn pink. "I know it's my job and it's sort of a nightmare to lock everything up but—"

"Lucinda," I cut her off with a wave and a grin. "It's fine. I'll take care of it. Besides, I owe you for the coffee," I say with a wink as I take a sip. "Is Bobby still here cleaning?"

"Oh," she breathes. "Thank you. My grandson has a T-ball game and I don't want to miss it. Bobby left about ten minutes before you got here. It's just you and Miss Greenwood."

"I can handle locking up. I'm only scheduled for the counseling session for an hour. I can't do too much damage to the church in that time," I tease and then sip on my hot saving grace.

She blanches. "Oh, Easton, don't even joke about that."

Laughing, I wave her on. "It's fine. Scout's honor. Now stop fretting and go. Boss's orders."

"Thank you. I'll send her in and then be on my way." Lucinda shuffles back out of my office and closes the door behind her.

I lean back in my chair and scrub at my scruffy face. I'll need to shave for tomorrow morning's sermon but I didn't have the energy this morning. Getting drunk with my buddies when I have work the next day not only left a queasy feeling in my gut but it also had guilt gnawing at me. It's difficult to walk the straight and narrow for Christ, but even preachers are sinners. I wish I had the strength in certain situations to remember my calling. But sometimes, it's easy to slip into sin and forget who I am. I always regret it the next morning and spend longer than usual in prayer asking for forgiveness and strength. A physically strong man like myself is often weak in the heart, no matter how hard I try to change it otherwise.

While I wait for Miss Greenwood, I pick up the file I started on her. Part of my duty as church pastor is to provide free Christian counseling to those in need. After I was released from prison, I was led by the church to get my license to become a preacher. I'd taught Bible classes while incarcerated, due to Tom's guidance, and finished my college degree in counseling. Dad's church had lost their pastor and the congregation had dwindled to hardly a few folks. They thought having someone younger and with some life experiences could build the church up again. I'm proud to say we have two-hundred eighty-six members and growing.

I love what I was called to do.

I'm fulfilled in a way drugs, sex, or sinful ways could never do.

When I'm doing God's work, I know I'm making a difference. I'm guiding those who are lost to him and making the world a better place.

I spoke with Miss Greenwood's mother, Stephanie, several weeks ago over the phone. Apparently, her daughter had gotten mixed up with the guidance counselor at her school at the beginning of the school year. He went to prison for sleeping with several of his underage students—many of which were non-consensual. Sadly, for Miss Greenwood, he'd knocked her up. She'd carried the baby for a month or two before she lost it. The poor girl seemed to spiral out from there and even got herself involved with an abusive drug dealer at her school. Once she hit rock bottom, Stephanie wanted to help her get her life back together.

In comes me.

While being a church pastor wasn't exactly what I set out to do in this life, it's what fulfills me for now. I like helping people in need. I love guiding them back to the right path. Once, I was out of control too and nearly ruined my life. Had I not had the law, family, and friends trying to set me straight, who knows, I could have ended up dead. Like my brother.

God has a plan.

And his plan for me is this.

A soft knock on my door jolts me from my inner thoughts and I close the folder. I place my Bible on top of it before clearing my throat. "Come in."

The door creaks open and a leggy blonde steps inside my office. For a moment, my eyes are glued to her honey-colored legs that extend from beneath a pair of skimpy white cotton shorts. She wears a pair of white Chucks and an ankle bracelet shimmers as it reflects the sun shining in behind me. When I find the sense to stop looking at her legs, I jerk my gaze up past her narrow hips and waist but linger on the swell of her breasts that are barely encased in a bright yellow camisole. I can see her nipples beneath the fabric for crying out loud. Long blonde waves hang down in front of her bare shoulders. My gaze pauses at her glossy pink lips that wear a small smirk.

Dammit.

I clear my throat again and meet her smug blue-eyed gaze. A golden eyebrow is arched in question.

"Hey, Preach."

I shake away my stupor and clench my jaw. Standing before me is high school senior, Lacy Greenwood. Her mother said she was troubled. She's trouble all right. But what has me all flustered is how easily—in one simple moment—I forgot who I was. A pastor. Instead, I roamed her body like a man does a woman when interested in her.

And that's just plain stupid.

I'm just a guy and sometimes I'm not immune to an attractive woman.

Now that I'm aware that she's indeed pretty, I

can put that behind me and move on.

"Pastor Easton McAvoy," I reply with a gentle smile. "Please, Miss Greenwood, take a seat." My voice is husky and I don't stand to greet her because then my inappropriate erection would be on full display. I'm irritated that I don't have more self-control.

I say a quick prayer for strength. God has helped me through tougher moments in life, surely he'll get me through this one. I certainly owe it to him to be on my best behavior too. When I was at rock bottom and alone, it was the love and forgiveness of Christ that pulled me through.

She saunters over to the chair and gracefully sits down. Her eyes take in my rugged appearance as heat flashes in her eyes.

Dammit. Dammit. Dammit.

Dane and Rick would be warning me right about now:

God is going to strike you down right here because your cock is hungry for this girl.

I rub the back of my neck and clear my throat. Again. "Your mother tells me you've had quite a year."

Her smug grin quivers right off her face. Heartache flashes in her pretty blues and she looks down at her lap. "Yep."

I sit up in my chair and shake away the lust that's attempting to prevent me from doing my job. My mind is still trapped in the past. That's my reasoning as to why I'm failing at finding my focus. I need to get back to the present. Where I'm a Godly man. A leader of the church. Someone who vowed to both God and the church that I would take a harder path than most to lead people to Jesus. "That's what I'm here for. To talk about it."

She swallows and shrugs her shoulders without meeting my gaze. "I don't want to talk about it but my mother is making me come here."

Leaning forward, I rest my elbows on my desk and try to meet her stare. "Lacy," I rumble, my tone commanding. "Look at me."

Her blue eyes lift and for a moment, I'm given a window into her soul. She truly is broken. The girl is strong on the outside but she's dying on the inside.

"Everything is going to get better. I promise." I give her a supportive smile. "Now tell me where it all started. Was it with Mr. Polk?"

Her golden brows furrow together and the tip of her nose turns pink. "I thought he loved me."

I feel sympathy for her. She's just a kid and some

old prick took advantage of her. He was supposed to guide and counsel her. Instead, he preyed upon her. "Go on."

She swallows and lets out a heavy sigh. "He didn't though. Apparently he slept with lots of girls. I fell for it. I fell for all his stupid words and soft kisses. We had sex." She watches me to gauge my reaction. Of course she won't find one. After being in prison for eight years of my life starting when I was just eighteen, it takes a lot more than a little sex talk to get me rattled. Once she realizes I'm not flipping out, she continues. "I had sex with him and then I turned up pregnant." A strangled sound escapes her. "It…I…" Tears leak down her pink cheeks and slip down to her jaw. I want to swipe them from her porcelain skin—which alarms me—but instead, I nudge the box of tissues her way.

"I heard he went to prison," I tell her. "And where did that leave you?"

She yanks a tissue from the box and dabs at her skin. Her bloodshot blue eyes find mine, imploring me to understand whatever is going on inside her head. "I was alone and pregnant. But I was happy."

"No shame in that. Babies are a blessing from God."

Her nostrils flare as she glares at me. "I must have been really bad because he stole his blessing back. He stole Mikey from me."

Reading her passages from The Bible to help her get past her grief isn't what she needs right now. I know better than that. Having helped many other convicted felons while they dealt with their demons, I know people need to be listened to and not preached at. Tom taught me that. When I was wallowing in self-pity, he listened and then he gave his advice. Eventually, he became a vital person in my life. A second father. A best friend and mentor. In due time, I can show her the verses that will help mend her heart just as he did with me.

"God doesn't work that way," I tell her quietly. "After your loss, what happened?"

She sniffles and shrugs. "I was broken and devastated. My happiness had been destroyed. I wanted to forget. Met up with a guy named Nolan Jenkins. I learned quickly which pills helped you forget. However, he presented new problems. Nolan was abusive." Shame flickers in her eyes. "I didn't know what to do. I fell out of one bad situation into the next. I'm terrible at picking out the right guys. All my friends seem to hook up with these wonderful, adoring men. And I get what's leftover."

I regard her with a frown. "Perhaps you should focus on your own happiness for a while. Happiness that doesn't revolve around finding a guy. What do you like to do for fun, Lacy?"

Her blue eyes gaze past me to the window. She's lost. So damn lost. "I don't know."

Pulling out a sticky note, I scribble down my phone number and a scripture: ***He gives strength to the weary and increases the power of the weak. (Isaiah 40:29).***

"Think about what makes you happy. Text them to me no matter how small or seemingly unimportant. I'll compile a list for you next session we have. You're going to get stronger and get through these difficult times, I promise. The list will help you find some direction. Will you come into the sanctuary and pray with me?"

She nods and stands. I follow suit and round my desk. Her eyes skim over my dress shirt before she tears her gaze away. I lead the way past Lucinda's empty desk and down the foyer hallway. Inside the sanctuary, the wood has recently been polished by Bobby and the smell of lemony pine is strong. Striding down the aisle, I take us straight for the pulpit. I motion for her to sit down on the steps and I sit beside her.

"Take a moment with your head bowed to acknowledge your loss and then we'll pray." My voice is soft and reassuring.

She bows her head and her blonde hair curtains around her face. I take the stolen moment to stare at her. Golden strands shimmer in her silky hair. The urge to run my fingers through her gorgeous mane is overwhelming but I grit my teeth and refrain.

"Let's join hands and say a prayer," I murmur, my voice low and gravelly.

She offers her tiny hands to me. Mine swallow hers. I grip her gently and begin praying. While I pray for peace and strength and love for this poor girl, I find myself silently praying for me too.

Self-control.

Patience.

Strength.

My mind is traveling down paths that don't have any business inside a church. I'll need to get a handle on my masculine desires because this girl needs actual help. She's been taken advantage by once before—by someone who was supposed to do the very thing I'm tasked with doing.

But I'm stronger than him.

I will not be seduced by the pouty-lipped vixen.

I'm going to help her, come hell or high water.

TWO

Lacy

"Amen," I repeat as I reopen my eyes.

His greenish blue eyes are narrowed. Our hands are still conjoined and neither of us makes any moves to pull away. I'm still stunned that the church counselor my mother set me up to meet with was so hot. After me falling for Sean Polk, I'm surprised she allowed this. You'd have to be blind to not think Easton McAvoy was attractive.

A strong, chiseled jaw that wears a bit of brown scruff with hints of red mixed in. Full lips that beg to be kissed. Strong nose with a few freckles sprinkled over it like toppings on a delicious sundae. But the best part of him is his hair. It's cropped short on the sides and longer on top. It's a dark brown but when the sun hits it, I see a hint of auburn shining through.

After a squeeze to my hands, he releases them and rises. I stand up next to this giant preacher. I'd heard rumors about him. That he did almost a decade in the penitentiary. I'm not sure for what. His eyes seem kind but the man has a body of a beast. My throat heats as I follow him up the aisle. His dark jeans hug his tight ass and his shoulders are broad. He's more muscular than lean but not in a meathead kind of way. In the way that would suggest he could toss you over his shoulder and spank your ass if you misbehaved kind of way.

Once we're in the foyer, his eyes travel my way. I don't miss the way his gaze skims over my body. Hell, most men can't help but stare. And I'd be lying if I said I didn't like it. With Sean, I'd loved the attention. He was older and said dirty things. I liked him a lot. Then, I thought I loved him. In my teenage brain, I was sure he'd kick his girlfriend to the curb and marry me. That we'd raise our baby together. But everything blew up and I was alone. When I lost Mikey, I was more than alone.

"Hey," Easton murmurs, his voice a low growl. "You okay?"

I blink away the tears and nod. "I'll be okay."

He stares at me for a beat longer as though he doesn't believe me but then stalks toward his office where I left my purse. I fold the sticky note with his number and slip it into my purse. He's gathering his things when my phone buzzes.

Mom: Hey, sweetie. Your Aunt Kimmie showed up with the boys. They've brought out the water balloons and are making a huge mess. Can you ask Pastor McAvoy to run you home?

Irritation bubbles in my chest. Aunt Kimmie and her boys are obnoxious. They always show up when Aunt Kimmie needs money. After eating everything in the house and letting her six-year-old twins destroy everything they come in contact with, they leave at least a thousand dollars richer. Mom just can't tell her sister no ever. And nine times out of ten, Mom abandons me to deal with them. Just like now.

"Uh," I start but then my eyes dart over to Easton as he picks up his helmet. "Never mind."

His brows furrow together as he studies me. "Lying in the house of God is a sin."

My neck and cheeks blaze bright red. “W-What?”

He flashes me a panty melting grin. “I’m teasing, Lacy. What’s up?”

“It’s nothing. Same time next week?”

His gaze is soft as he regards me but eventually nods. “Don’t forget to start your list.”

I give him a forced smile and rush from his office. As soon as I step outside, I wish I’d worn a little more clothing. Old habits. Once the school skank, always the school skank. Holding my head high, I start the long journey by foot home. The skies are darkening in the direction I’m headed which only makes me more frustrated with Mom and Aunt Kimmie. I make it a good half mile when I hear the rumble of an engine. The sound is chased off by rumbling thunder ahead of me. When the first raindrop hits my head, I groan.

I’m thankful I wore my Chucks and start running. The rain is now splattering me faster and harder. I’ve hardly made it very far when the sound of an engine roars behind me. One peek over my shoulder tells me that Easton McAvoy is coming to save the day on a loud motorcycle. I’d seen the helmet on his desk but seeing it on his head as he powers through the rain with the bike between his thighs is quite a sight. A sight that makes my heart skip in my chest.

"Get on," he barks as he pulls off his helmet. The rain soaks his handsome face and his shirt now molds to his sculpted body. His blue-green eyes are imploring me to take the helmet. As much as this feels like a bad idea, I can't help the tiny thrill that shoots through me as I push his helmet on over my head. It smells like him. A masculine mix of cologne and peppermint. The water pings off the helmet but I'm thankful for a reprieve.

"Careful for the exhaust pipe. It'll burn your leg," he warns as I straddle the bike behind him. I wrap my arms around his solid middle and have to swallow down the excitement surging through me. My core that's pressed right up against his ass throbs. He gives my knee a little pat. "Hold on tight."

I squeeze him and let out a yelp when he gasses the bike. He doesn't go very fast on account of the rain but the drops ping painfully against my flesh anyway. I'm shivering and miserable, so much so, that I realize I haven't told him where I live. He turns down a street into a modest neighborhood and drives to the end. We come to a stop in front of a house that sits mostly by itself. He pulls the bike under a covered carport and kills the engine.

"It's not safe to ride in the rain. I figured you could hang out here until it passes and then I'll drive you home," he says, his voice husky. Lightning cracks and I shriek. "Come on, honey, let's get you inside."

He climbs off and then offers me his hand. I'm warmed by the fact that he helps me off the bike before removing the helmet. His gaze roams down my front before he stalks over to the door that goes into the house. He murmurs prayers under his breath but I hear them. *Lord, give me strength.* I follow him inside and I'm immediately impressed with his small home. For one, it smells good. I thought guys had gross houses. Sean's house smelled like sweaty socks. Easton's house smells like oranges and cinnamon.

"Are you cooking something?" I ask as I shiver. My teeth clatter together.

He stares at me for a beat too long. Anguish flickers in his gaze and I immediately somehow feel responsible for the look. It's as though he's struggling. Guilt nags at me because as much as I want him to like me, I don't want him to feel as though it pains him. "My mom brings me this wax stuff that you melt and it makes your house smell good. Don't ask me how it works. Every couple of weeks she comes and switches it out for me."

I laugh but then my teeth start chattering again.

"Come on," he says, the pain in his eyes fading away as compassion floods in. "I've got something for you to wear." This time, it's me who stares for too long. His eyes are beautiful. Unlike Sean who had evil intentions in his gaze, Easton's eyes are gentle and good. He feels safe. Like the type of person who knows exactly the right things to say and just when you need a hug, he'd be the first to give it. Despite his rough exterior, love for his church and God are worn proudly upon his shoulders and in his kind gaze. It's evident he takes pride in what he does. "This way."

Following him through his house toward his bedroom feels naughty. A thousand dirty images flit through my mind. Images where the preacher pleasures the girl with his mouth. I bite on my lip to suppress the moan that rumbles in my chest. He strides over to a dresser and pulls out a white undershirt, a pair of white socks, and a grey pair of sweatpants.

"There's a bathroom in the hall you can change in. Leave your clothes in there and I'll toss them in the dryer." He flashes me a warm smile. "You like coffee? I'm afraid I don't have much else to offer you."

I don't tell him I hate coffee. When I was fourteen, I got it in my head that I would drink some of

Mom's black coffee. It was nasty and I vowed never to drink it again. I simply nod and fumble along until I'm in the bathroom. One glance in the mirror and I'm mortified. My hair is a frizzy soaked mess. The mascara I'd put on is smeared beneath my eyes and my lips are slightly purple from the cold. I look terrible. Of course he looked good enough to eat in his rain-soaked dress shirt that molded to his carved from stone body.

After peeling off my soaked clothes, I put on the dry ones that smell just like him. They're huge and hang from my body. Even after tying the sweatpants as tight as they'll go, they still slide down my hips. At least the socks are warm. I can't do a thing about my hair but I do manage to clean away the smeared mascara. When I finally emerge from the bathroom, I find him in the kitchen making coffee.

He hands me a Harley mug and I frown to see the coffee is more of a tan color than black. His gaze is on me, almost expectantly, so I bring the steaming cup to my lips. Each time he stares at me, heat floods through my body. A nervous, excited kind of heat. *Lacy, do not crush on your preacher. Just because you like to screw up your life, don't mess with his.*

I take a tiny sip. "Oh," I mutter in surprise. "This

is actually yummy."

A boyish grin turns up one side of his lips. It positively melts me from the inside out. So much for not crushing on the preacher. "I figured judging by the look on your face when I mentioned coffee that you weren't a black kind of girl. Lots of cream and sugar. Is it sweet enough for you?"

He's talking about coffee and here I am imagining dirty things. Again. All I can do is nod before stealing another tasty sip.

Don't crush on him. Don't do it.

"Hold on just a sec," I tell him as I set down the mug. I rush back to the bathroom where I abandoned my things and fish out my phone from my purse. I tap out to the number I was given.

Me: Easton's coffee makes me happy.

I'm just walking back to the kitchen when I hear his booming laughter. When I round the corner, he's staring at his phone with a smirk on his lips.

"That's a great start, Lacy." His eyes twinkle with warmth. I wonder how to turn that warmth into heat—like the heat that has begun to burn in my belly.

Lacy, he's good and he's your preacher. Enough with the girlish crushes.

We sit down at the bar in his kitchen and I shiver when his knee brushes against mine.

"I heard you were in prison once," I mutter. When I chance a glance his way, his gaze darkens.

"I made some mistakes. We all do."

Because I've always been one to push by nature, I prod at his answer. "What sort of mistakes?"

Shame causes his cheeks to turn pink. "Young, stupid ones. I got involved with the wrong crowd. Trusted people I shouldn't have. When they asked me to run some drugs to a friend's out of state, I did it because it was good money." He runs his fingers through his soaked hair and a strand falls in front of his eye. It gives him a dangerous look. "I got pulled over. Despite being a first-time offender, the amount of coke I had in my trunk had me looking at eight years."

I frown and my heart clenches. Easton is a good guy who made a dumb mistake. It changed the course of his life forever.

Kind of like me.

Before I can stop myself, I reach up and brush the hair from his eye. His greenish blue eyes darken to more blue than green as he glares at me. The glare isn't an angry one though. It's as though he's attracted to me and it's taking everything in him not to maul me.

And he can't maul me.

At least, I'm pretty sure he *won't* maul me.

The fact that I'm in his space, a blonde little temptation, has guilt once again making my skin crawl. Why can't I flirt with a guy my own age and with someone who isn't bound to the church? It makes me as evil as Sean for wanting something I shouldn't. I shudder and Easton frowns as though he worries I'm cold. I smile quickly and sip more coffee.

"Did you serve all eight years?"

He looks away, breaking our stare, and takes a sip of his coffee. I feel like I wait forever before he speaks again.

"I did ten, vixen."

Vixen?

Letting that comment slide for the moment, I gape at him. "Ten? How come?"

"Early on, I was angry. I'd abandoned God after growing up in the church, and didn't know how to cope with my emotions. I was just an eighteen-year-old kid looking at eight years in prison. When some bigger guys thought they would teach me a prison lesson in the showers, I lost my head. Whatever they tried to do didn't happen. But I ended up putting three of them in the hospital. I sort of blacked out with rage. To this day, I still don't remember."

"Oh…" I swallow down a sip of my coffee to formulate my thoughts. "So they added some time?"

"Five more years. Luckily, not long into my sentence, I cleaned up and got right with God. Stayed on the straight and narrow. Thanks to my friend Tom." His eyes flicker from fondness to sorrow. It breaks my heart for him.

"Did something happen to him?" I whisper, my voice shaky. I don't want him to be sad but I want to know more about him. He's learned so much about me so far that I feel like it's only fair.

"He died of a heart attack. For six years, Tom studied The Bible with me each day and prayed with me. My hardened heart was no longer something dirty and ugly. With his help, I'd polished it into something worthy and shiny. His approach was tough—tougher than my own dad—but that's what I needed. And when I got out of line, he'd thump me in the head. I think I still have bruises," he says, chuckling.

I smile too. "I'm sorry about your friend. So they let you out early?"

"My reviews after that initial screw up were all stellar. I was allowed to work on my college degree and ministered some to the other inmates thanks to Tom's teaching and guidance. They let me off three years early."

Ten years in the penitentiary.

Wow.

"How long have you been out?"

"A decade. I'm at peace now. The anger at my friends and myself are long gone."

I work out the math in my head. He's thirty-eight. Same age as my dad had he lived that long. Heat creeps up my neck. "I'm sorry that happened."

He smiles and it's reassuring. "It made me who I am today. I'm stronger because of it." He stands from the bar stool and clutches my shoulder. His thumb is dangerously close to my breast. "I'd planned to watch *The Walking Dead* marathon today. If you're not in any hurry, you're welcome to hang out and watch."

I laugh and it feels strange. Lately, I don't do much laughing at all. "*The Walking Dead*? Preachers can like zombies?"

He smirks and I swear my insides combust. "Who says we *can't* like zombies?"

THREE

EASTON

I HAVE NO IDEA WHAT I'M DOING. NONE whatsoever. But inviting her back to my place and giving her my clothes seems like the worst possible idea ever.

Guilt.

It's a familiar feeling. One that I've not had to deal with for quite some time. While in prison, I'd felt guilt for how I'd blamed my father. Tom helped me understand that Elias was troubled. There was nothing any of us could have done. We loved him and that was all we could do. Once I shed some of the anger, I'd wanted nothing more than to do right by my father. The first letter was the hardest to write. But every letter after got easier. It got easier because he wrote me back. His letters were filled with love, compassion, and guidance. He even expressed his own sorrows and guilt. It was as though on paper, he could truly open up to me. I felt closer to my father than I ever had been as we slowly fumbled our way to each other.

And now, after all these years, guilt is once again nagging at me. I shouldn't have brought Lacy here with me. But something about her begged to be comforted and cared for. She needed a friend. Someone she could count on. Being there for someone is Christ's way. But the darker thoughts roaming in my head are sinful. They're far from Christlike. I keep repeating prayers in my head but they get scrambled every time she speaks. My mind isn't pure right now. There's a tugging in my heart that I'm unfamiliar with. That, coupled with the guilt, has my mind spinning with every reason why having her here is wrong.

For one, the white shirt doesn't hide her nipples very well and they poke through the fabric begging to be seen and tasted. *God give me strength.* The last thing I need is to stare at this teenager's breasts all afternoon. And yet, here I am. Stealing glances whenever she's not looking. It's dirty and wrong. Sinful. Shameful as hell. It's fitting that my sermon tomorrow is outlined to talk about temptation.

Is God tempting me to see how I'll handle the situation?

I'm strong.

If I could survive a decade behind bars, I can sure as hell survive this.

She follows me into the living room. I turn it on to the station and kill the lights in the room. With the storm going on outside, it makes for a good day to watch zombies on TV. I sit down on the sofa, offering her the recliner, but she plops down beside me. She drags the crocheted blanket Mom made while I was in prison down into her lap and leans into my shoulder.

"It's cold."

I laugh and lean back against the sofa. "That blanket is the warmest one I own. You'll be hot within minutes."

Her eyes widen at my choice of words. I silently curse myself for how they could be misconstrued.

"Just watch the show," I murmur, my voice hoarse.

We watch for three back-to-back episodes. Lacy's never seen the show before and had lots of questions. I patiently answered them all. And when she wasn't asking questions, my mind was repeating scriptures about strength. I thought about how I'd deliver the sermon tomorrow. With passion and vigor. Yet, the guilt was still there eating away at me.

When we first sat down on the sofa, we'd both been stiff and awkward. Now, she lies on her side with her cheek on the armrest and her legs in my lap. I don't know how we got into this dangerous position but neither of us has made any moves to change that. And now, I can't get my mind to recall one single Bible passage in my head. All I can feel is how warm her feet are on my thigh.

My phone buzzes and I chuckle.

Lacy: The Walking Dead makes me happy.

Our eyes meet and hers are flickering with happiness just like she mentioned. It's nice seeing the sadness gone from her pretty blues.

Me: Coffee and TWD. A girl after my own heart.

It's meant to be a joke but as soon as I send it, I feel stupid. Her cheeks burn bright red. I'm giving her the wrong message.

Lacy: I call dibs on Daryl.

I laugh and the tense moment evaporates. From the app on my phone, I order us some pizza but then find myself drifting off to sleep. After last night's bar hopping, I'm exhausted.

I wake with a start. I'm on my side with my cheek pressed against Lacy's ribs. Her fingers are resting in my hair. It wouldn't be so bad—even with her legs sprawled out over my thighs—except that I have my hand on her bare flesh.

One quick look and I'm frozen. The sweatpants she borrowed are pulled low on her hips. Her hip-bones are showing and the area from her belly button down to the waistband of the pants seems like a huge naked divide. My palm is possessively splayed out on that part of real estate as though I own it. The thought of letting my lips own her there too has my cock jumping in my pants. Her skin is warm beneath my touch and I startle myself when my thumb caresses it. For one moment, I'm just Easton and she's some sweet girl—a girl I'm quickly losing my mind to.

I'm still trying to figure out what to do when the doorbell rings. My gaze snaps up to Lacy's and I find her staring at me sleepy eyed. Her eyes are soft and not filled with terror like mine.

I'm a preacher.

Christ has called me to do something good and impactful. I won't let him, my family, or my congregation down. I won't let this innocent girl down either by giving in to my lustful urges that have no place in my heart.

"You should answer that," she murmurs, her voice raspy from sleep.

I grit my teeth. Despite all my internal pep talks, my body is still responding to her nearness. Dammit. Now I have to answer the door with a ten-inch boner on full display. I choke down my unease and launch myself away from her. By the time I've answered the door and paid for the pizza, my cock has settled.

We're quiet as we eat but Lacy begins tapping away on her phone. Already, I'm hoping it's a text for me. When my phone buzzes, I flash her a grin.

Lacy: Cuddles and pizza make me happy.

Sweet, adorable damn girl. I don't even think she realizes just how tempting she is. A little vixen with a pouty mouth and breasts of a grown woman. She's messing with my head. My head is screaming at me to remember who I am. Pastor Easton McAvoy.

Yet my heart…

It's confusing me.

Thump after wild thump of my heart, I find it harder and harder to latch onto my vows I made to God. It's as though her scent fills my nostrils and intoxicates me. Tempts and slowly destroys me. I'm going to have to seriously get myself together. I may even need to pray with my dad to find my way again.

And this?

Her. My house. Cuddling.

This can't ever happen again.

"Eat up," I tell her, my voice raw with a need for something I'll never allow myself to have. "Rain has stopped. Time to go home."

Lacy: The piano makes me happy. I didn't realize how much I missed playing it.

Lacy: Mom's laugh makes me happy. She's so beautiful when she smiles.

Lacy: OMG. Coach Long's AP Calculus class makes me happy…when it's over.

Lacy: Quiet Friday nights alone make me happy.

Lacy: Listening to you on Sundays as you

preach makes me happy.

Lacy: Our Saturday TWD dates make me happy.

It's been almost two months since I started helping Lacy. And my gallant efforts to not put myself in a tempting situation were thwarted. Each Saturday, I invite her over. A talk with my dad and extra prayers, though, have helped me get my focus back. I'm able to ignore my body's cravings for hers and instead reach out to her heart. It's been broken and through Christ's love, I want to be the one to help mend it. At first, she didn't talk much. But since then, we've peeled away her childhood. All of her broken relationships. Her feeling of abandonment by her best friend Olivia. Worries over her future. The guilt she feels, even though she shouldn't, about Sean Polk being in prison. The one we don't talk about much is the loss of Mikey.

"How far along were you?"

My words catch her by surprise and she stops mid-chew. The commercials during the episode are loud, so I hit the mute button. She swallows and picks her purse up from the floor. I watch her dig around until she finds her wallet. Inside is a folded photograph. When she hands it to me, I learn that it's a sonogram picture.

"Thirteen weeks." Her voice cracks. "I don't know what the sex was but my heart tells me it was a boy. So I named him Mikey."

I study the grainy picture and wonder how that must have felt for her. She wears the grief and sorrow always just under her surface. It makes my chest ache for her. When I hand the photo back to her, our fingers brush against one another. Our Saturday dates aren't ones I tell anyone about, not even my dad. After her session with me each week and a prayer, we always come to my house after. As friends, of course. But it's getting harder to ignore the way my skin buzzes whenever she's near. Or the way my heart skips in my chest when she laughs. No amount of prayer can counteract the physical way my body reacts to her.

I drag my gaze to the television as I try to work out my thoughts. I'm not sure what the hell I'm doing with this girl but it's not right. Besides the fact that I'm willingly disobeying God's will and everything I stand for, there's more to the situation than that. She's underage and I'm a convicted felon. It's a recipe for disaster. And yet, I can't help but want to spend time with her. For the first time since I've been out, I've felt a connection with someone. I had a connection with Tom. A father of sorts. We were inseparable until the Lord called him home. But now, the lonely ache that gnaws at me has lessened. There's a person who wants to spend time with me just as much as I want to spend time with her.

My phone buzzes beside me and I eagerly pick it up. I've come to love knowing what makes her happy.

Lacy: This makes me happy.

I frown and glance over at her. She's lying back against the arm of the sofa and her legs are sprawled out across me. Since today is hot, she's not covered in the blanket. The light green summer dress hugs her body in a delicious way. The hem of it is on the shorter side and rides so far up her thighs that I get a peek at her white panties beneath. My cock is instantly hard. I grit my teeth and try to look away but I can't. Today, she's too damn pretty.

I close my eyes for a moment and say a quick prayer.

You're stronger than this, Easton.

And I am. But the moment I open my eyes, they

dart greedily back over to her.

Her lashes are painted dark with mascara and they bat innocently against the tops of her cheeks. She's wearing a shiny pink lip gloss that makes her lips seem plumper and more bitable than usual. And her hair—God that hair—is down today in soft, silky waves. Without thinking, I reach over and toy with a golden strand that sits just above her breast.

"This makes me happy too," I tell her. I'm honest to a fault sometimes. I should be telling her she's getting the wrong ideas and that this can't happen—whatever *this* is. And yet, all I can do is secretly revel in the fact that she's happy with me.

Her breath hitches when I release the strand and run my thumb across her bottom lip. Once my mind catches up to my action, I jerk my hand away and lean my head back against the sofa. My heart is hammering in my chest. It's been ages since I've been with a woman. So long in fact, I can't even remember. I may be a pastor, but I'm not perfect. I've slipped a time or two and slept with a woman over the years out of wedlock. God wants you to hold out and wait for marriage but sometimes the sinner within doesn't care. That sinner just wants someone to hold.

I'm lucky my God is a forgiving one.

I have much to be forgiven for.

"Sean wasn't good to me," she murmurs, drawing me away from my inner turmoil. My gaze slides between her thighs once more and I'm both elated and disturbed to see her panties again. Her dress isn't hiding them anymore. Instead of scolding her, I fixate on the wet spot that darkens the fabric. I lick my lips and jerk my eyes to hers.

"He was a bad man," I agree.

She frowns. "I mean, he said all the right things in the heat of the moment but…" Her throat bobs as she swallows. "We never had anything like *this*."

I want to chastise her and tell her we don't *have* anything. But again, I'm not a liar. This connection that has burned between us since the moment she stepped into my office is all I can think about. This connection has me up late at night stroking my cock as I imagine all kinds of sinful images with the young teenage blonde on my couch and then fervently begging God for forgiveness.

"Lacy…" My words die in my throat when she takes my hand and threads her fingers with mine.

"Yeah, Preach?"

I laugh and it eases some of the tension from

my muscles. "You know what we're doing isn't right. Something as innocent as hanging out as friends…" I trail off and run my fingers through my hair with my free hand. "It's too tempting. I'm no better than Sean. Bringing you here is unethical and wrong." *And the things I imagine doing to you aren't Godly.*

She squeezes our linked hands. "Why is this wrong, Easton?"

"For one, your mother would kill me. Two, I hate the idea of anyone taking advantage of you. Including me. And three…" I groan. "I could go back to prison. I'm not looking to do that again anytime soon. Although, it would give me the opportunity to kick Sean Polk's ass for hurting you."

Her giggles have me smiling too. "Preachers can't say ass."

"Says who?" I demand with a grin.

"I don't know? God?"

"God's less concerned about my cussing and more concerned with…" *The way I keep staring at the wet spot on your panties and wondering what it tastes like.* "He's just more concerned with *this*."

"*This*," she repeats. "God doesn't want you to be happy?"

I bring our conjoined hands to my mouth and

kiss the back of hers. "Honestly, Lace, I don't know. There's nothing in Scripture that will guide me through *this*."

"I seriously doubt The Bible says you can't date," she murmurs. "That you can't fall in love. Isn't that what ninety percent of The Bible is? Love thy neighbors and whatnot?" She draws her knee up to rest her foot on my thigh. This forces her dress to reveal more of her panties. The little vixen knows what she's doing. She's pushing me further and further toward the edge. Even Jesus was tempted. But his heart was much stronger than mine. The sinner ingrained in me begs to indulge.

"Honey," I start, my voice husky. "I can't. As much as I want to, I can't."

"Can't what? Like me? Don't you do that already?"

I squeeze her hand and kiss her knuckles again. "I definitely like you. More than I ever should."

"So what's the problem then?" she whispers, her blue eyes flickering with self-doubt. I want to squash that look in her eyes. She should never doubt how perfect she is. Just not perfect for me.

"The problem," I growl as I do the unthinkable and run my fingertip along the wet spot on her panties. "*This* is the problem."

Her body jolts at my touch. "It doesn't feel like a problem to me." Those words come out as a soft murmur.

Oh, God.

What am I doing?

I grasp for verses inside my head but nothing makes sense. Only her. My mind is quiet as she seems to sing a song I'm aching to hear.

I bend my finger and take to running my knuckle along the wet fabric. "The problem is once I start, I won't stop. I know this with every part of my being."

She lets out a whimper of pleasure. "Nobody's asking you to stop."

I'm hanging on by a very thin thread here. My cock is aching and hard. It's almost painful against my jeans in its attempt to escape. As if she's attuned to my thoughts, she rubs her foot along my shaft. It jolts in response and I let out a choked grunt.

"Dammit, vixen," I snarl.

Self-control is snapping.

Snap. Snap. Snap.

The sinner in me is winning. He's desperate for her.

"Easton," she moans. "That feels good."

Damn right it feels good. I could do so many things that would rock her world. Things that Sean Polk could never have dreamed of.

Stop that train of thought, Easton.

You're a man of God. Her mentor. A friend.

I murmur a silent prayer for strength but it's hard to stay focused when each time my knuckle rubs against her clit, she moans in such a delicious way that I want to press my mouth against hers and suck the sound right into my throat.

Her foot keeps teasing my cock. Our linked hands grip each other tightly. My lips kiss each of her knuckles over and over again.

"Please," she begs, her voice strained. Her eyes have fluttered closed and her teeth bite down on her fat bottom lip as she writhes against my knuckle. "Easton, please."

"We can't do this," I groan.

Can't.

Can't.

Can't.

"Please."

Dear God those pleas are going to make me lose my mind.

"Lacy."

"Easton…"

Her panties get wetter and wetter. Images of me pushing my cock inside of her tight body nearly make me go insane with need. I'm lost. So many times I've preached sermons on those who were lost and finding their way to God. I feel as though I'm spinning out of control and I can't seem to focus on him. Will I ever find my way back?

All it would take would be for me to push her panties to the side and slip my finger inside her tight channel. That would be the catalyst for destruction. It would satisfy the both of us. I'd forsake everything I've worked hard for and prayed for. My destiny and calling would be blown away with one simple act. The only thing keeping this all from happening is the very wet, very thin piece of fabric between us. And yet…I haven't even kissed her supple lips. I'm three seconds from fingering her and I haven't even tasted that pouty mouth.

I'm no better than Sean Polk.

And I'm a disappointment to God.

Jerking my hand from between her thighs, I let out a pained growl. Her arousal, such a sweet scent, permeates the air. I lick my lips because I'm so damn hungry for her.

Please, Lord, give me strength. I beg of you. I'm blinded by lust and the needs of the flesh. I don't want to sin against you. I don't want to go down this path because I'm afraid there won't be any coming back.

"Why'd you stop?" she breathes, her brows crushed together as if she's physically hurting.

"I can't."

She sits up and straddles my lap. Her pink mouth is parted and inviting. I want to nibble on that lip. I want to suck on it, dammit. My hands remain fisted at my sides. If I touch her, I won't stop.

Please, Lord.

Her fingers slide into my hair and she takes the lead. With slow, fluid movements, she rocks against my throbbing hard-on. The way she grinds against me feels so good. I'll come in my pants like a loser if she keeps at it. Her hot breath tickles mine when she runs her nose along mine.

"Kiss me, Preach."

I close my eyes because as much as I want to do that, I can't. "No."

"Easton…"

"No."

Her lips brush against mine and I'm tempted once more. I want to devour this girl. *She's jailbait.* I grit my teeth but a groan escapes me the faster she moves her hips. Each movement feels amazing on my cock.

"It can be our secret."

God will know. God always knows.

"I'll know," I growl. "It's not right."

She stops moving and stares at me with a trembling lip. "I thought I finally found a good one. And he doesn't even want me." Lacy is far from manipulative. This is exactly how she feels right now. It kills me that I'm responsible for hurting her right now.

"Lacy," I start but she sits up on her knees to move away. "Lacy stop." My hands grip her waist and I urge her to sit back down.

Her blue eyes are wide as she blinks at me in confusion.

"I want you so bad," I admit, shame coating my voice. "But if I start this…If I kiss your pretty mouth like I'm dying to…" I swallow. "I don't know what happens with my life. And honestly, that scares the hell out of me."

She breaks eye contact and looks down between us. My massive hands dwarf her narrow waist. I like having her in my grip. I like it too damn much.

"I'll be legally old enough this summer," she

murmurs. "That's close enough."

I give her hips a squeeze. "I wish it were now. That would make this decision a lot easier."

A smile tugs at her perfect mouth. "You'd have sex with me if I weren't jailbait?"

I look up at her and smirk. "I'd do more than have sex with you. I'd blow your mind, vixen." But then I grow serious again. "And it's more than that. I've made a promise to God and *this* breaks that vow."

"God will forgive us," she whispers, the sounds speaking straight to my cock. Her lips curl into a beautiful smile and damn is she ever gorgeous. "Kissing's not a crime though."

"Kissing is a tease. It'll start something I can't finish."

Her dark lashes flutter as she nods, defeated. I've never seen a more perfect person. Her skin is flawless—the color of honey. I know she runs track at school and her body reflects that of a runner. Lean and lithe and tanned from the sun. She has breasts that would bring most men to their knees in worship. I'm certainly not immune. In a matter of two months, this girl has rocked the very foundation I stand upon. She makes me question my future and want to forget my past.

"Lacy," I start. Her blue eyes dart to mine. My God is she vulnerable as hell. "I care about you. More than I should. You deserve someone who could parade you around on his arm. I wouldn't be that person for you."

She cups my cheeks and frowns. "I don't want to be paraded around. Easton, I just want to be loved." I close my eyes when she presses a soft kiss to my mouth. So innocent and sweet. Just like her. When she doesn't move away, I groan. My palm finds her jaw. I have every intention of pushing her away.

But then I'm not.

I'm pulling on her jaw to open her to me. Like a gift just for me. The moment a surprised sound escapes her, I steal it. I steal it right from her mouth. My tongue slides past her lips and meets hers greedily. It takes her a moment to realize I've given in to kissing her because she lets out a moan and deepens the kiss. Her fingers slide back into my hair and she kisses me hard. I nearly die from pleasure each time she grinds against my cock that is begging for attention. I lose myself to the moment and slide my palms down from her waist to the tops of her bare thighs. Her breath hitches when I slide them back up under her dress.

"You're addictive," I murmur against her mouth. "I told you one kiss wouldn't be enough."

She whimpers and nods. "I want more too."

We kiss hard again and then my thumb is rubbing along the side of her panties where it meets her thigh. I brush my thumb past the edge and back over her clit. Over and over again, I massage her over her panties as we kiss. The sounds coming from her are downright erotic. They have me aching for so much more than this. Even the few times I lost my head and had unattached sex while in my position as pastor, it never felt like this. The craving to be with someone was never this intense.

"Easton," she cries out.

And then she's exploding.

Lord, please forgive me.

FOUR

Lacy

I'M EMBARRASSED TO SAY THAT DESPITE ALL THE times I'd been with Sean, he'd yet to make me come. Ever. At the time, I was just so happy to be with him. I thought asking for an orgasm was selfish. What was selfish was him demanding sex whenever he had a free moment from his fiancée. Quick. Sloppy. And only one person came. It all was worth it though when I got pregnant. It felt right. I loved that baby as soon as I peed on that pregnancy stick. Mom, despite crying and being disappointed, promised to help me raise the child.

But then Sean went to prison and I lost Mikey.

Looking back, I realize hindsight is much clearer. Sean wasn't good to me. He used me. I was naïve and desperate. Fell right into his trap.

Easton though…I've never felt like this before. Sure, I'd fooled around with boys before ever sleeping with Sean but not once had they made me feel like this. Not once did they make me come with just their thumb without even going past my panties.

Easton drives me mad.

He speaks to parts of me that I thought died when I lost Mikey.

Easton is different.

My eyes open to find him staring at me. The heat and hunger in his eyes is overpowering me. I want to beg for him to carry me into his room and make love to me. I open my mouth to ask him for just this when my phone starts ringing.

It breaks the spell and I hate it.

I don't like the panic in his blue-green eyes that are the color of the Atlantic Ocean we often visit for summer vacations. All the intensity that he'd just looked upon me with is gone. Guilt morphs his features and I'm saddened that he looks that way. What God frowns upon two souls connecting? It's pure and heartfelt, that much I am certain. Nothing about this feels sinful. I wish I could erase the look on his face and make him realize this.

"You should answer that," he says gruffly. His hands grip my hips and he effortlessly moves me out of his lap. When he stands, I can see just how aroused he is by the bulge in his jeans. "Lace. Answer your phone."

I blink away my daze. "Hello?" I greet breathlessly.

"Lacy, sweetheart, where are you?"

Oh, crap. Mom.

"Uh," I stammer out. "J-Just hanging out watching *The Walking Dead* with a friend." Not a lie. Easton stalks out of the room and I feel sick to my stomach. "What's up?"

"We're going to dinner tonight with Aunt Kimmie and the boys. I'll come get you. Just send me the address."

I panic and let out a shrieked response. "Mom! No. I'll meet you there. Where?"

She hollers to Aunt Kimmie. "You still want Chinese?"

"Yep!"

"Moon Wok. You know where that is? Downtown near our attorney's office? Remember, sweetheart?" she asks.

I know exactly where Moon Wok is. After many visits to see my lawyer, Mr. Alexander, we would often go in and eat at Moon Wok. I'm glad the entire Sean Polk drama is over.

"I'll be there in twenty minutes," I agree with a sigh.

"Love you, Lacy Lou."

"Love you too, Mom."

When I hang up, I find Easton at the end of the sofa with his keys in one hand and his helmet in the other. His features are stormy, as though he's regretting touching me. I stand up from the couch and take the helmet from him.

"I have to go," I whisper.

His jaw clenches and he won't meet my gaze. "I know. We should head out."

I place a palm on his chest and look up at him with pinched brows. "Are you mad at me?"

His intense eyes dart to mine. "I could never be mad at you, Lace. I'm mad at myself."

Hot tears well in my eyes. "Why?"

"Because we kissed…because I touched you…" He huffs. "I've messed up. I'm sorry."

I blink away my tears. "Sorry for what?"

"It won't happen again," he assures me as if he isn't breaking my heart with those words. "Let's go."

I hurry and jerk the helmet on so he doesn't see me cry. After I snag my purse, I follow him out to the bike. He fires up the engine and climbs on. Once I'm settled in behind him, my boobs smashed against his back, he takes off. A couple of times his palm caresses my outer thigh but then as if he remembers he's not supposed to touch me, he jerks his hand away. It's confusing and makes me sick to my stomach. By the time he pulls up outside of Moon Wok, I have zero appetite.

I climb off the bike and smooth out my dress. Then, I pluck off the helmet and hand it to him. His gaze bores into me for a long moment.

"I'll see you at church tomorrow." His eyes dart up to the heavens above. "I have much to be forgiven for."

"Easton…"

"Bye, Lacy."

I nod and give him a small wave before he's gone.

"Who was that hottie?" Aunt Kimmie questions from just outside the restaurant door, a cigarette dangling from her bright orange lips.

"Uh…a friend."

"I never had friends like that in high school. Maybe if I did, I would have got knocked up a lot sooner." She snorts at her joke. It only leaves a sour taste in my mouth. Makes me think about Mikey. He might have been conceived by a mistake but I never thought of him that way. I wanted him.

Ignoring her, I stomp past her and find my mom in the restaurant. Aunt Kimmie is on my heels, chattering on about finding a sugar daddy while my tits are still nice. Poor Mom is trying to corral Aunt Kimmie's bad twins, Jimmie and Johnnie as they try to scoop the koi out of the fountain in the middle of the restaurant. Why she agreed to go to dinner with these nuts is beyond me.

"Boys, that's enough," my aunt barks at them. "Go sit down."

They grumble but surprisingly obey. My mom lets out a breath of relief. Everyone says we look just alike. Mom is almost forty but she looks young for her age. Dad's been dead since I was three and she's always put taking care of me first. Even before dating or anything else. The men are certainly interested in Mom though. I've had teachers at my school ask me for her number before. Gross.

"I missed you, sweetheart." She pulls me in for a hug and she smells lovely today. I wish I could speak to her about Easton but I'm afraid she will see it as another Sean Polk situation. It couldn't be farther from that if it tried.

"Missed you too."

Aunt Kimmie snorts. "She wasn't missing you too much. Don't let the girl lie to you. You should have seen her boyfriend. Built like a linebacker and drove a motorcycle."

My face blazes with heat.

"What?" Mom asks in astonishment, hurt lacing her tone. I've always been able to share things with her. Aside from Sean and Easton, I've always been upfront with her. She knew the first time I let a boy touch me and gave me the longest lecture known to man about the birds and the bees. But she did it out of love. I know this.

"He's not my boyfriend," I bite out, shooting Aunt Kimmie a scathing glare. "Trust me, Mom."

Her gaze softens and she strokes my hair. "But you want him to be."

I give her a weak smile. "Yeah."

"Where'd you meet him? Better yet, when do I get to meet him?" she questions as we take our seat.

I wave her off. "Mom, I told you, he's not my boyfriend. I met him at church."

Her blue eyes brighten as she grins. "I knew you were going every Sunday and Wednesday night but I had no idea you met someone there. How wonderful. That's a great place to meet boys. They don't have expectations of a sweet girl like yourself."

I flinch. The only one with expectations is me. And this boy is a man. "Yeah."

"It's settled then. I'm coming with you tomorrow. I haven't been to church since your Dad was alive." She beams at me. "It'll also give me a chance to meet Pastor McAvoy. I'd like to chat with him and see how your counseling is going."

All I can manage is a nod. Thankfully Mom gets distracted with Jimmie when he spills his soda all over the table. I take the moment to text Easton.

Me: My mom makes me happy.

He replies immediately.

Preach: I'll add it to the list.

I bite on my bottom lip as I type.

Me: She's coming to church tomorrow.

It takes him ten minutes to respond.

Preach: I'd love to meet her.

That's it. We don't discuss the kiss or him making

me come. Nothing. Even as my mother hugs me from the side and babbles on about her job happily, I still can't help the lonely feeling that has settled at the pit of my belly.

Why must my life be so complicated?

Mom sings along to all the hymns beside me and listens to Easton's sermon attentively. Normally, I enjoy our togetherness but today it leaves me on edge. I tossed and turned all night thinking about the kisses Easton and I shared. I'm afraid the dynamics of our relationship have changed. He's hardly cast a glance my way the entire morning. I daze out, not listening to him preach, as I stare boldly at him. Today he's handsome as ever. He's shaved his face smooth and his brown hair is tousled on top of his head. It reminds me of how it was last night after I ran my fingers through it.

He's so gorgeous. You'd have to be blind to not see it.

I catch a woman in the choir staring at me. Her brown hair is curled and she has kind eyes. Familiar kind eyes. I'm stunned for a moment as I realize she must be Easton's mother. Feeling guilty, I tear my gaze from the pulpit and stare at the Bible he gifted me the second weekend I met with him. He'd highlighted some passages he wanted me to read. Quickly, I flip through them—anything to take my mind off the woman watching me watch her son. Eventually, I get caught up reading and it isn't until my mom touches my shoulder do I realize people are leaving.

"I can see why you enjoy coming," she says. "Pastor McAvoy has a way with keeping your attention."

I stand and follow her out of the pew. "He's good at what he does," I agree.

"So show me this boy you like," she whispers, her eyes scanning the congregation that's laughing and talking as they leave. "Was it the blond boy who kept looking over here?"

Blond boy?

All I saw the entire sermon was Easton.

He's all I ever see.

"Uh…" I start but my words die when said blond boy saunters over to me with a goofy grin on his face. Bobby, the church's janitor, watches intently from the pew the boy came from. They have similar eyes and it makes me wonder if they're siblings.

"Hey," he greets, his cheeks slightly pink as though he's embarrassed.

Mom pats my shoulder. "Sweetheart, I'm going to go catch up with Pastor McAvoy. I'll leave you two alone."

She abandons me with this stranger whom she thinks I like. I mean, had I never encountered Easton, perhaps I could have been into someone like the guy in front of me. He's tall and cute and wears an endearing smile. But he's not…

"I'm Bryce."

He holds his hand out to me and I reluctantly take it. My gaze skims the sea of people until I find a pair of familiar blue-green eyes. Easton's jaw ticks even as he attempts to smile at my mother. I don't miss the flicker of jealousy in his eyes. It makes my heart stutter.

"Nice to meet you," I murmur as I drag my attention back to Bryce. "I'm Lacy."

He opens his mouth to speak when a woman clutches my elbow.

"Excuse me," the woman says, her voice sweet and warm. "Can I get your help finding candles for tonight's service?"

I turn my head to regard her and almost flinch

when I stare into the same eyes Easton has. "Um, yeah. Of course."

"Bye, sugar," she says to Bryce before guiding me down the aisle, her grip never leaving my elbow. "Tell Bobby and your parents I said hi." I'm worried she knows about Easton and I. Is she taking me away to yell at me?

We pass by Easton who frowns at us in confusion and then she ushers me down the foyer. It isn't until we push through his office door that I really begin to feel nervous. The woman closes the door behind her and then sheds her choir robe.

"Lacy Greenwood?"

I nod at her, a stupid stare on my face. "I am."

She smiles at me as she opens a cabinet and hunts for a coat hanger. "I'm Lydia McAvoy, Easton's mother." Once she hangs her robe up, she closes the cabinet and turns my way. Her eyes are narrowed as she scrutinizes me. "Easton's a good man."

I freeze at her words. "Preachers usually are."

She smirks. "You're a guarded girl, aren't you?"

"I don't know what you mean."

She picks at imaginary lint on the shoulder of my dress. "You keep secrets tucked away and not many people know the real you."

I blink at her in confusion. “I don’t have secrets.”

“Good answer. Especially when those secrets involve my boy.” She lets out a sigh. “Listen, he’s a good man. Problem is, he wears his heart on his sleeve. I’ve been watching the two of you for a couple of months now. I’ve noticed the attraction. The pull. And then, after this weekend, the tension. Something happened. I prodded Easton before church and he blew me off but his eyes don’t lie. Just like yours don’t either.”

“I…I…”

“You’re not quite old enough to legally date my son, darling. And while I don’t approve of my son’s choice in desiring a woman so young, I can’t stop him. I’m also not one to talk. I fell for his father when I was fifteen. We married by the time I was your age.” She smiles fondly. “All I’m saying is that I wanted to get you alone so that I could see for myself what has my boy all flustered. I see it. You’re gorgeous and quiet and mature compared to others your age. You’ve been through some difficult times. My only request is that you don’t hurt him. That you please don’t do anything to put him in a position that could get him into trouble or fired from the church.”

“Of course,” I choke out.

"Also," she says with a sigh. "Stay clear of the Johnston boys. Bobby isn't right after the accident and Bryce…" Her lips press into a firm line. "I've heard unsavory things about him."

I nod. "Okay."

"When's your birthday?"

"June eleventh."

"Come by June twelfth for dinner. You and Easton. As a couple. Gregory, my husband, would be charmed to officially meet you as well, I'm sure."

I'm still gaping at her when Easton barges into the office with Mom on his heels. Mom's babbling on about colleges or something but he's not listening. His eyes find mine. Concern is painted on his features when he sees my shocked expression and his mother beaming.

"Sorry to interrupt," he grumbles.

"Oh, sweetheart, you interrupted nothing," Lydia says. "You must be Lacy's mother. I'm Lydia, Easton's mom. My do you two look like sisters or what?"

Mom chuckles. "We get that a lot. I'm Stephanie Greenwood."

"That's a beautiful dress. Kate Spade?" Lydia asks as she motions at my mom.

"The Target knockoff. Lacy shows me where I can find good style at half the price. My girl is a great shopper," Mom explains.

"This is fun and all but I'd like to speak to Lacy alone for a moment. Can you take this riveting conversation into the hallway?" Easton deadpans.

Lydia laughs. "Little snot. Fine. Come on, Stephanie. Let's go grab a cup of coffee from the kitchen."

As soon as they leave, Easton prowls over to me. He looks handsome in his charcoal grey suit and thin dark grey tie. I want to slide my palms up his hard chest and kiss him. Instead, I stay rooted to the floor.

"Your mom says you're seeing Bryce Johnston." His eyebrow lifts in question.

"And your mom wants us to come for dinner on June twelfth."

We blink at each other for a long moment before he cracks a smile. I can't help but smile back.

"I'm not seeing Bryce. You know this," I murmur.

His palm finds my cheek and he brushes his thumb across my bottom lip in a bold way. "I do know this. What I don't know is why Mom is inviting us to dinner."

"It's the day after my birthday," I say with a huff.

Understanding flickers in his gaze. "Ahhh, I see. That was Mom's way of approving of you."

I let out a choked sound. "What?"

"She likes you."

"She intimidates me," I breathe. "She's all beautiful and intense."

"And protective," he quips. "And intuitive."

"Are we really that obvious?" I ask, heat burning up my neck.

"I didn't think so but apparently we are."

I frown. "Not like it matters anymore."

He leans in and my heart rate skitters. "Why's that?"

"Because you made it clear that we *can't*." I throw his word back at him.

His palm slides to my neck and he clutches me in a possessive way that makes my skin buzz. "Maybe we *can*." The torment—a never ending war—flickers in his gaze but he blinks it away as he stares at me in appreciation.

"What?"

He doesn't reply but instead presses his lips to mine. The kiss is sweet but makes a statement.

When he pulls away, he murmurs, "I didn't like seeing you sad today. And when that kid was holding your hand, I wanted to pry him away from you." He takes my hand in his. "I'm not going to lie, I'm struggling because of my position here at the church and betraying my calling, but this is mine." He squeezes my hand.

I melt at his words and then let out a moan when he kisses me deeply. After thinking all night he was done with me, I was wrong. Easton McAvoy does want me. Guilt tugs at my heart about how he's feeling but it only wants me to try and assure him that this decision is a good one.

The door pushes open and we wrench apart. He doesn't let go of my hand though.

"In Jesus' name," he says. "Amen."

"Amen," I squeak.

He releases my hand and we both turn to see my mom. She glares at him for a moment but when I smile at her, she softens.

"You ready to head out, sweetie?"

I nod and shoot Easton a quick glance. His eyes are burning with need and promise and maybe even slight indecision. The stare he gives me is far too intense to share in the presence of my mother.

"See you at next Saturday's session," I chirp to Easton as I leave.

"I'll be looking forward to it, Miss Greenwood."

His words make me blush and I nearly stumble over my own two feet on the way out the door.

FIVE

EASTON

Lacy: Tacos make me happy.

Lacy: Running makes me happy.

Lacy: OMG…Chris Pine makes me happy. Swoon.

Lacy: Looking at old pictures of my dad and I make me happy.

Lacy: Music makes me happy.

Lacy: Thinking about our kisses make me happy.

"What are you so happy about?" Dane asks me, a smirk on his face as he sips his beer.

I stuff my phone in my pocket and shrug. "Just

helping one of the church members."

He arches a dark brow. "By the smug look on your face, I'm going to assume this member is a chick. Am I right?"

Laughing, I tilt my beer up to my lips and speak before drinking. "You might be right."

"Fucking right, I am," he says with a crooked grin.

"What are *you* so damn happy about anyway?" I counter.

"I'm seeing someone." His gaze drifts out the window. "It's serious."

"I figured after your divorce, you'd be ready for anything but serious."

He scratches his jaw and pins me with a firm stare. "This is different. This is real."

As he rambles on about a client of his, my mind drifts to Lacy. She's definitely different. And my God is she real. I can't get her scent out of my nose or her laugh out of my head. It's been five days since I've seen her. With school and running track, she stays busy. I'm supposed to see her tomorrow morning per usual but suddenly I don't want to wait.

"I think I'm going to head out," I tell my friend. "Catch you for lunch one day this week?"

"Quinn's going to meet me Tuesday for burgers. You should come then."

I slap some bills on the table beside my hardly touched beer and saunter out of the bar to my bike. After I straddle it, I text Lacy back.

Me: You make me happy.

The dots move as she replies.

Lacy: Seeing you would make me happy.

Me: I don't think your mom would approve.

Lacy: Mom is at a movie with my aunt and nephews. They left about thirty minutes ago. You could come visit…that is if you wanted to.

My heart thumps in my chest. I miss her and want to hold her.

Me: Text me the address. I'm on my way.

Twenty minutes later and I pull up to a fancy house on the outskirts of town. The lawn isn't as neatly kept as the neighbors' but the home itself is. My loud Harley rumbles through the streets making me feel extremely out of place. I guess a middle-aged preacher calling on a teenage girl is what seals the deal though.

Once in front of her house, I kill the engine, leave my helmet sitting on the seat and trot up to her front door. Before I can raise my hand to knock, it swings open.

Jesus, give me strength.

Standing before me is an angel. An angel I want to undress and worship. One I want to taste and touch.

She's wearing an oversized sweatshirt that hangs off one shoulder baring her creamy skin and no bra strap. But what has my cock waking up and interested, is the fact that she doesn't seem to be wearing pants. The sweatshirt barely covers the tops of her thighs. If she were to lift her arms, I wonder if I'd be able to see her panties.

"You going to stand there staring all day?" she teases, her hand on her hip and a smirk tugging at her plump juicy lips.

Okay, so coming here was a bad idea.

A very bad idea.

"Come here," I growl as I reach for her hand. I pull her to me for a friendly hug. But there's nothing friendly about the way my hands cup her ass over her sweatshirt. She hugs me tight and I squeeze her bottom tighter.

"Getting a little handsy there, Preach," she teases, her voice light and playful. "You'll give all the neighbors a reason to want to come to church. I mean, if you're giving that kind of show…"

I pop her on her ass with both hands before pulling away. "Does that mouth ever get you in trouble?"

Her lips twitch. "Only always." She reaches for my hand. "Come on. I want to show you something."

She leads me inside and heat seems to burn from the place she's touching me. I groan when we head upstairs toward a bedroom. As soon as we step into the girly room, I know it's hers.

"Sit down," she says softly. "I won't bite. You look nervous." She laughs. "You haven't sinned yet, Preach."

I let out a deep breath and sit on the edge of her bed. She walks over to her desk and pulls out a notebook. When she comes back, she sits close enough to me that our thighs touch. I'm thrown back to when I was fifteen and had a girl in my bedroom for the first time. I keep listening for sounds—just waiting to get caught by my parents.

"I made this. For Mikey." She swallows and looks at me with teary eyes. "It's…It's probably stupid but it helps."

I take the notebook and lean forward to press a soft kiss at the corner of her lips. Her breath hitches. I want to kiss her hard but I want to see what's in the book more. She's revealing a part of herself to me.

Leaning away from her, I open the book. As I start to read, I quickly discover she's written a fictional piece about a boy and his mother. He's clever and funny and rowdy. She adores him. Reads him stories and they pretend they're dinosaurs. It's both heartbreaking and beautiful all at once. She's written many chapters. I read them quietly for a good half hour as she sniffles. Every now and again, I reach over and squeeze her hand. Once I reach the end of her story, I regard her with a solemn stare.

"This is really nice, Lace." And it is. Not only is it emotional and powerful but it's well-written too. Her handwriting is neat and I can tell she took great care in writing this story. "Are you going to finish it?"

She takes the book from me and nods. "I started it after you and I met that first time. I wanted to honor Mikey doing something I love."

"I didn't know you liked writing," I admit. It's another piece of her that she has shielded from the outside world.

"Mom says you can't make a living writing," she says with a laugh.

I shrug. "I don't know. I read some pretty stupid

books while in prison. They weren't half as good as this."

Her cheeks turn pink and she gives me a shy smile. "Really?"

The self-doubt she carries around with her like a mountain of armor is something I want to help her drop. She's beautiful and smart and funny. There should never be any doubt whatsoever about her talents.

"Really." I slide my palm to her throat and run my thumb along her jaw. "I'm going to kiss you now."

She laughs as my lips connect with hers. The kiss is playful and flirty at first. But soon, our tongues are dueling for control. I grab her narrow hips and drag her into my lap. She straddles my thighs while my palms grip her bottom. The way she grinds against me has me needing more from her. My palms slide up under her shirt and I'm met with bare flesh.

"Lacy," I growl. "Where are your panties?"

She moans against my mouth. "Last time they were in the way. I didn't want them in the way this time."

With this girl, all sanity is gone. I'm betraying my oath to live as sin free as possible and instead turning all that off to be with her. I'm not strong at all. I'm weak. I'm also a convicted felon with a rap sheet a mile long. Just because I'm a preacher and friends with the sheriff doesn't mean I should be flirting with the law and chasing what's illegal.

And yet, I want her.

In this bedroom, just the two of us, it's easy to forget that there are rules that prevent two people like us from being together.

"God, you're beautiful," I murmur against her plump lips. "So tempting and perfect."

She whimpers when I squeeze her ass. I want to touch her—all of her.

"This shirt has to go," I snarl a little harshly. I grip the bottom and pull away to stare at her blazing blue eyes. "I'm going to take this off and touch you. If you don't want that, now's the time to tell me, vixen."

She bites on her bottom lip and nods. "I want you to touch me."

The sounds coming from me are feral and animalistic. My morals have taken a back seat as this starved man attempts to devour this young woman. I pull her shirt away from her body and toss it away. Fat, juicy tits stare me in the face. Her nipples are hard little stones, the softest pink I've ever seen.

"Just look at you, dammit," I growl. "An angel."

She looks down between us and a smile plays on her lips. "I could get on my knees—" A shriek rips from her when I flip us around and lie her on her back on the bed. With her legs spread, I'm able to control the friction between us.

"I like you beneath me for the time being. You can get on your knees later," I murmur as my lips find her throat. A low moan purrs from her as I suck on her flesh.

Lord, forgive me for what I'm about to do.

"Are we going to have sex?" she asks, her voice breathless.

"Right now we're just kissing," I growl and nip at her skin. "Don't rush me, vixen."

I bite her and kiss her slowly down her neck to her collarbone. The moans coming from her are loud and ragged. I've barely touched her. I bet she's a screamer. My cock strains against my jeans at the thought of her shouting my name in ecstasy.

When my mouth begins kissing the top of her breast, she squirms. Her movements get wilder the moment I latch on to her nipple. I suck hard enough to make her cry out and then I lazily tease the flesh to calm it down.

"These nipples taste delicious as hell, Lacy."

She grips at my hair. "You're teasing me."

I meet her gaze as I pull her nipple between my teeth and tug. I pull hard enough to make her cry out before letting go. "Teasing is half the fun."

Slowly, I kiss and suck her sweet skin down her tight stomach past her belly button. When I reach her pubic bone that's been shaved bare, I growl against her flesh. "I like this. I like this a helluva lot."

She doesn't have a chance to respond because then my mouth is on her. Damn is she ever sweet. Her clit is hot against my tongue and I'm about to make it burn. Slowly, I rub circles around it as I tease the opening of her pussy with the tip of my finger. My little vixen is dripping with need. I love how wet she gets for me. It makes me want to bury my nose against her clit and drive my tongue deep inside her to lick it all away.

"Oh, God," she moans. "Oh, God."

I suck her clit into my mouth as I push my finger into her tight hole. Her body lifts from the bed as she screams. My cock is throbbing almost painfully with the thought of driving deep inside of her. I've been with few women since my release but none have had such a ripe body as Lacy has.

"My cock is going to feel even better stretching your pretty pussy out, Lace," I murmur before nipping at her clit.

She cries out and thrashes and then my sweet girl is coming hard. As though she's possessed by the devil, she convulses with jerky movements. Her pussy clamps tight around my finger and I know she's going to feel so damn good when I come inside of her. Juice runs from her body and my finger makes a slurping sound as it slides in and out of her. When she's done losing her mind, I suck on her tender clit once more before pulling away.

I stare at her for a long moment as I slip my finger from inside her. Her cheeks are rosy red and her throat matches the color. Wild blonde hair is in messy tangles around her. And the bluest eyes I've ever seen regard me with wonder beneath her thick, black lashes. I roam my gaze over the swells of her perfect young tits down to the pussy I just devoured. I'm admiring the way her sex glistens in the overhead light when I hear her sniffle.

Jerking my gaze up to her face, I'm confused to see her lip trembling. I practically pounce on her and cradle her cheek with my palm. Tears well like tiny blue lakes ready to spill past their dams.

"What's wrong, baby?" I press a kiss to her nose that's now pink. "Did I hurt you?"

A sob escapes her and she shakes her head. "N-No. It was perfect. Nobody…I mean…"

I kiss her mouth before frowning at her. "Nobody what?"

Glassy tears slide down her temples like a waterfall. "Nobody has ever pleasured me before. And they've certainly never looked at me the way you just did…as though I'm perfect and beautiful and desired."

I stare at her as I study her gorgeous features. Lacy is beautiful inside and out. She deserves someone who will be good to her all the time. I want to be that man, despite the timing. I want her to know how she should be treated. With adoration and respect.

"You're all those things and more. Those other guys were assholes," I growl.

She laughs and runs her fingers through my hair. "I was so giving. I…" Another tear slips out as shame dances across her face. "I was a skank."

I scowl. "You weren't a skank."

She swallows. "I'm embarrassed for you to know how many boys I fooled around with."

"I'll kill them all." I'm only half joking.

Her lips curl up into a smile. “I only ever slept with Sean though. But…”

I press my thumb to her lips. “I don’t care if you gave everyone at your school a blow job. People can change, Lace. You’ve changed. Life threw some pretty hard stuff at you and you survived. Here you are living—and doing one helluva good job at it I might add. Stop beating yourself up over your past and start living for your future.”

She pulls me closer and our mouths meet again. I devour her in a desperate way. This girl does things to my mind—things no other woman has before. Our relationship isn’t right, I know this. I’m supposed to be guiding her through her rough times, not guiding my dick roughly into her. I need to be the adult. The responsible one. The Godly one. And yet…I don’t want to, dammit. I want to claim her and worship her. I want to throw everything away for a few stolen moments with her.

“Easton,” she whimpers. “I need you.”

I tear away from her mouth that is red and swollen from my attack. Christ, she looks hot with my mark on her. I growl as I fumble with unfastening my jeans. They get shoved down my hips but before I can get my boxers down, the craving to kiss her mouth wins out. I pounce on her again and our lips connect as though they were made to fuse together one day. But now without my jeans in the way, I can feel every curve of her wet pussy through my boxers. We both groan at how good it feels.

"Take them off," she begs. "I need you inside me."

I'm dizzied with desire and desperate to push my cock inside of her. "The pill. Tell me you're on the pill."

She whimpers. "No. I've never been able to take the pill or any birth control for that matter. I get sick from them." Her blue eyes are wild and frantic. "Tell me you have condoms."

I close my eyes. A slew of curse words are barely contained in my mouth. "No. I'm not exactly sleeping around with anyone and haven't been for a while."

"Nooo," she whines. "No."

I laugh against her lips. "This is messed up."

"Completely," she agrees.

"I guess I'll just have to make you come again like this," I breathe against her mouth. I rock against her in a way that makes her moan.

"Yes," she chokes out. "Just like that."

With each stroke against her, my boxers slide further down my hips. The tip of my cock touches her flesh causing us to both hiss out air.

"Rub it against me, Preach. Without your stupid boxers in the way. You can come on my stomach," she says, her tone desperate.

She doesn't have to tell me twice. I shove my boxers down my thighs and free my throbbing dick. When I slide it against her clit, we both make strangled sounds of pleasure.

"T-That feels good," she cries out. "Don't stop."

I thrust against her slowly, careful to run my length between the lips of her pussy along her clit. I'm dying to slip it lower and push inside her but I know myself. I wouldn't stop. I'd drive into her until I came all up inside her. That would screw both our lives up in an instant.

"You're worth it," I grunt out as I buck against her. My teeth tug at her bottom lip. "You're worth whatever consequences come after this. Worth straying from my calling." I bite her lip again. "You're mine, Lace. Not that kid from church. Not the asshole who hurt you. Mine."

My words send her over the edge and she shatters beneath me. The way she shudders without any control to her movements is the hottest thing I've ever seen. With a roar, I spill my seed all over her lower stomach. My sticky cum soaks her and the bed below her as it runs down her sides.

One day I'm going to come inside of her.

The thought is feral and possessive. I don't know what to make of it. What I do know is that I want that. I want to spread her apart and mark her from the inside. The very thought of anyone touching her ever again is enough to make me want to kill every asshole who she comes in contact with.

I want her to come home with me.

Now.

"Lace—"

Her phone starts buzzing and her eyes widen. "Oh, crap! What time is it?"

"Almost ten," I say after a quick look at my watch.

"Oh, God. That's Mom. They're probably on their way home," she squeaks.

I roll off her and watch her tiny ass jiggle as she scrambles to answer her phone. Her cheeks are bright red and my cum runs down the crease of her pussy. Damn, she's hot.

"Hey, Mom," she chirps. "Oh. Ohhh. Umm…"

She waves at me and her eyes are panicked. "I like Rocky Road. Cherry Garcia is my fave though. No, you don't have to turn back. Mom…Mom."

She mouths to me. *You need to leave.*

Disappointment that matches the look on her face ripples through me. I slide off the bed and tuck my flaccid, wet cock back into my boxers and jeans. She's chattering to her mom as she tries to turn her sweatshirt inside out to put back on. I take it from her and fix it.

"See you in a few. Bye."

She hangs up and yanks the shirt over her head. "Oh, God. I'm so sorry. They are at the corner store not far away picking up some pints of ice cream. She'll be here any minute. I can't believe I lost track of time." Her bottom lip juts out and I know I need it. Stalking over to her, I grab her jaw in my grip and kiss her hard. When she's calm and breathless, I pull away.

"Tomorrow. We continue this tomorrow."

I've never seen her smile more beautifully.

SIX

Lacy

I'M STILL HIGH FROM LAST NIGHT. EASTON WAS IN my room and we were together. It was so much more than anything I ever had with Sean. For one, Easton is attuned to my feelings and mood. He's not simply trying to get in my pants but he honestly likes me. When he'd gone down on me, I nearly lost my mind. I'd never experienced anything quite like it.

"You're in a daze there, sweetheart," Mom says as she parks the car in front of the church. "Everything okay?"

I was frantic and flustered when she got home last night. Easton had barely driven off when they passed each other on the road. It was too close of a call for my liking. I love my mom and she's pretty cool but something tells me she'd flip out if she caught my preacher licking my pussy.

"It's fine. I'll sort it all out with Pastor McAvoy this morning," I tell her. At least I don't have to lie.

She takes my hand and kisses the back. "I love you, Lacy Lou. You know you can talk to your momma about anything. Anything." Her eyes flicker in a knowing way. It makes me wonder if Lydia said anything to her. Easton and I haven't had sex yet so there's technically nothing to talk about.

"Thanks, Mom. I love you too. When there's something to talk about, you'll be the first to know."

Her shoulders relax. "Okay. Just be careful. You've been through a lot."

I tear my gaze from hers because my mind drifts to Mikey and I don't want to cry in front of her. Easton isn't at the church yet but two cars are in the parking lot—Bobby and Lucinda. Waiting in his office is better than Mom probing about me wanting to have sex with my preacher.

"Bye, Mom. I'll see you later for dinner," I chirp, my tone slightly fake.

She grumbles. "Actually, I have to cancel.

Kimmie and I are driving out to your grandparents' house. We're going to stay the night and pack up their things. She found a nice mobile home to stay in near the house and she has an interview with Moon Wok. I'm just helping her get her life sorted a bit and then it'll be just us again, kiddo."

"Okay," I tell her as we hug. "I'm looking forward to some pedicures without Aunt Kimmie giving me a play-by-play on how to hook a sugar daddy."

Mom chuckles as we part. "Whatever advice Kimmie gives you, do the exact opposite."

"Deal."

I climb out of the car and wave to her as she drives off. I'm just starting for the door when Bobby comes out. Bobby isn't much older than me. I've learned from Easton that he graduated two years before me. Bobby had a scholarship to play football but then ruined it all by drinking and driving. The accident landed him wrapped around a pole. Luckily no one else was involved. But it did give him a head injury and he's not been the same ever since. Kind of spacy. Sometimes a wee bit creepy. Normal people don't stare and if they are staring, they look away when caught.

Bobby just stares blatantly.

Always.

It makes me think of how Lydia warned me about both him and his brother.

I look down at the sexy but sweet pale yellow dress I wore and silently curse myself. I'd worn it for Easton but I didn't consider that Bobby would get an eyeful too. And like the creep he is, he stares at me as he drags a rolling trashcan toward the dumpster—even craning his neck over his shoulder to check me out.

After giving him an awkward wave, I hurry over to the church doors. When I turn the handle, it doesn't open. I'm just swiveling to ask Bobby to let me in, when I hear footsteps come up on me. He's within inches from me which means he ran all the way over here. I let out a squeak of surprise and my ass bumps against the door.

"Hey, Lashey." He has a lisp too. I'm not sure if it was from complications of the accident or part of the head injury.

"Hey, Bobby. Can you let me in?"

His eyes scan over my face and he stares at my mouth. I can smell coffee on his breath. My inclination is to shove him away from me but I know he's different so I try not to panic. "You're pwetty," he says in adoration. "My brover thinks so too."

I give him a polite smile. My heart races when I hear the loud rumble of a familiar motorcycle. Bobby stands in my space and doesn't make any moves to step away. It isn't until the engine of the bike is cut off and two hands grip his shoulders that he moves. And that's because Easton physically guides him away from me.

"What are you two kids up to?" Easton asks, his tone playful. But since I know him well, I pick up on the edge in his voice.

"Lashey is pwetty and got locked ousside."

Easton grunts. "And you were just going to let this pretty lady stand out here all day?"

Bobby frowns but I wave it off. "It's fine. I'm feeling a little hot though. Can we go inside for our session?"

Easton fishes his keys out of his pocket and unlocks the door. With his palm on my lower back, he guides me inside. Bobby follows us all the way to Easton's office. Lucinda blanches when she sees Bobby creeping on us. Easton simply gives her a slight shake of his head before ushering me into his office.

"Bobby," he teases, "we don't pay you to stand

around. If you're all done, go on and head home."

Bobby's gaze lingers on me for a long moment before he nods. Easton closes the door, not waiting for him to leave. Once we're alone, Easton stalks over to me and hugs me to him. His lips find the top of my head in a sweet kiss.

"I don't want you alone with him. He's not all there, Lace," he warns, making me shiver. "Promise me you'll stay with your mom until I get here next time."

"I promise," I vow because quite frankly I don't want another repeat of that uncomfortable situation. "I have good news."

I tilt my head up and stare at his handsome face. Easton is the kind of man who looks too dirty and dangerous to be a man of God. Just seeing him on his bike on the street, you'd assume he was some thug or something. But when he's in the pulpit spouting off Bible verses with such passion, you can see what a good man he is. Looks can be deceiving. He may look like the devil on the outside—brutally sexy, chiseled jaw, piercing hot eyes, tattoos peeking out from beneath his rolled up shirtsleeves on his forearms—but he's a fierce angel.

"Tell me," he murmurs as his lips rain kisses

on my mouth.

I smile against his sweet assault. "Mom isn't coming home tonight. I thought maybe I could stay over."

His gaze darkens and he trails kisses to my ear. I gasp when he tugs at my lobe with his teeth. "I would love nothing more than to have you in my bed all night. And because I can't go through another moment like last night, I bought some of these too." He reaches into his pocket and retrieves a condom.

I laugh. "Look at you. Premeditating."

His palms find my ass through my dress and he squeezes. "You're mine now. I don't care if we have to be each other's dirty little secrets. *This* is happening."

I'm slightly disappointed that we have to hide something that feels natural and right from the outside world. But I'm not stupid either. I'm not legal yet and he's a convicted felon and a preacher. If that's not playing with fire, I don't know what is.

We start to kiss again when my phone buzzes. He pulls away and saunters over to his side of the desk. I want to grumble about having to have a session but truth is, I enjoy these talks with Easton. I get a lot off my chest. He never preaches at me or tells me what to do. He simply listens without judgment.

Once I sit down, I fish my phone out of my purse.

Jessie: You never RSVP'd. Coming out tonight to celebrate my birthday?

I groan. I'd been so wrapped up with Easton, I'd forgotten about my friend's shindig. We've been friends since grade school when the teachers used to confuse us as sisters but we drifted some this year. I know that's my fault. I got involved with Sean and then Nolan. Still, I'm not looking to reconnect after all this time and pass up an opportunity to spend the night with Easton.

Me: Happy birthday, Jess. I'll make it up to you. Just you and I can go to dinner one night. But I have something I can't miss tonight.

Not a lie.

I can't miss this if I want to keep my sanity.

Jessie: No worries. Courtney will be there and you know she likes to get crazy. I know you don't like her much but I still wanted to invite you.

Me: Be careful. Courtney's trouble. But then again, maybe you'll get arrested.

Jessie: That's the plan. Talk soon, babe.

I tuck my phone back in my purse to find Easton watching me with a smirk. God, he's hot. Today he picked out a white dress shirt that's rolled up to his elbows and the top two buttons are undone. It's slightly wrinkled but it somehow looks good on him. On Saturdays, his scruff is always grown out some before he shaves it all away for Sunday. I'm staring at his full lips when he clears his throat. A dark eyebrow arches in amusement.

"I know I'm good looking but maybe you should take a picture since it'll last longer and all," he jokes.

I laugh. "I prefer the real thing over a picture."

"Everything okay?" He gestures to my purse.

"Yeah. My friend wanted me to come out tonight for her birthday but I told her I had important plans. Plans I could not miss."

His sinful smile stretches across his face. "Those plans are extremely important, I agree." Then, as if slipping into preacher mode, he leans forward and opens his Bible. "I thought we could touch on some passages today about coping with loss."

All playfulness bleeds from me and I frown. "Joy."

"It worked for me," he says, his eyes flickering with sadness. His brows scrunch together as if he's in pain.

"Tom?"

His lips press into a firm line. "I was better equipped to deal with my feelings when he passed away. Actually, it was my brother."

I gape at him, my lip trembling. "I'm so sorry."

"It's what sent me spiraling. Elias was just two years older than me. I adored my big brother. Worshipped him, really. When he committed suicide, I was angry. I blamed my father. It took Tom's love and guidance to get me through the anger and sadness. Through the word of God, I was able to find peace." His expression is wistful. "It's why this," he motions around him and thumps his Bible, "is so important to me."

I bite on my bottom lip, guilt flooding through me. I'm responsible for him straying from God. Losing a brother has to feel every bit as awful as losing a child.

"Listen, I know you hate this," he murmurs, his tone soothing. "But it's just a part of it. Talking through these things and learning ways to deal with your sadness will help you feel better, Lace."

I nod and blink away tears. The tears are always just below the surface. All I have to do is think about what Mikey could have grown up to be and then they're slipping out of their hiding place, soaking me with my own sorrow. I don't realize I mentally checked out until two warm lips start kissing my knuckles. Easton kneels before me and has threaded our fingers together on one hand and is swiping tears from my jaw with the other.

I shake away my daze and frown. "I'm sorry."

"Nothing to be sorry for," he breathes, his lips brushing against my flesh.

We're quiet for a long time and then he kisses my bare knee. A ripple of pleasure shoots up my thigh to my core. When our eyes meet, his are smoldering. Neither of us speak as he slowly inches my dress up my thighs. His fingers disappear under the fabric and he latches onto my panties.

"Lift your bottom," he instructs, his tone husky.

I grab the arms of the chair and lift. He pulls my panties down to my knees. His fingers run across the inside and he growls.

"Always so wet for me," he utters, almost as if he's fascinated by that fact. But how could I not be wet? He's sex walking. A hot fantasy come to life. The bad boy turned good. I crave him with every ounce of my being.

"Only you," I promise.

His greenish blue eyes darken to mostly blue. “Damn straight.”

I smirk. “You can’t cuss in church.”

“I also,” he murmurs as his hand slips between my thighs, “can’t do this.” His finger pushes into me and I gasp. “But I’m doing it. When it comes to you, vixen, I want to do it all, consequences be damned.”

He curves his finger inside and presses against a sensitive place within me. I groan and writhe against his hand. When his thumb starts working my clit while his finger rubs me on the inside, I start to see stars.

Holy shit this feels good.

“Easton,” I rasp. “Oh, God.”

A knock on the door makes me want to scream.

“Everything okay in there?” Lucinda asks. “I can bring some tea.”

She thinks I’m crying. Oh, God, I’m going to start crying if she doesn’t go away.

“We’re fine,” Easton assures her, his fingers never losing their stride. “Nothing a little prayer can’t fix.”

“I hear that,” Lucinda says with a chuckle before we hear the squeak of her office chair when she sits back down.

Easton works me harder and faster until I'm unraveling.

"Jesus Christ!" I cry out when my orgasm rips through me.

"Amen," he growls.

I suppose to an outsider, it would seem we're deep in prayer. In reality, the preacher is just deep in *me*.

His finger slips from inside me and he makes a provocative show of licking my juices from his finger. The glare he's giving me is feral and positively evil. I get high off the look on his face. It makes me want to see it more often.

"Stand up," he orders in a low voice. "Bend over my desk. *This* can't wait."

I obey him but sway on shaky legs. He steadies me with his hands on my hips. The touch is gentle but then he roughly twists me away from him. With his strong hand on my back, he pushes me down across the desk. My ass is bared to him and I feel exposed. He runs the palm of his hand under my dress and I shiver when his fingers tease the crack of my ass.

"I'm going to make you mine, Lace. Right here. Right now. Any objections?"

"None," I breathe.

"Good girl," he murmurs. "Are you going to be quiet as a church mouse? That's the only way we can do this."

I nod. "So quiet."

He chuckles and gives my ass a squeeze. "But just in case…" His cock through his jeans presses against my backside as he leans into me. He dangles my panties in front of me. "Open."

I bite my lip for a moment before obeying. Gently, he pushes my panties into my mouth. Once I'm stuffed with them, he caresses my cheek and grins.

"You look so damn beautiful right now."

My eyes flutter at his compliment. He disappears from my line of sight and I shiver when he pushes my dress up my hips. His palms whisper over my ass before he removes them. When I hear the quiet buzz of his zipper coming down, I become antsy. He's so slow and so patient that it's driving me insane. The tear of the foil can barely be heard over my ragged breathing.

And then he's giving me what I want. Well, sort of. Slowly, he teases the tip of his cock against my opening but doesn't enter me. He slides his length up between the crack of my ass and then he pushes it down to rub between my thighs. I'm whimpering with need and wriggling when he finally pokes at my opening.

"Are you still wet for me, vixen?"

I moan and nod.

"Good girl," he praises. "Remember to be quiet."

I nod again but then I lose all sense of reality when he begins inching his way inside me. I've waited for this moment since pretty much the moment I met him two months ago so of course I'm dripping with need. He slides easily into me. My body stretches to accommodate his impressive thickness. I've only been with one other man and Easton's cock is a beast in comparison.

"Dammit," he hisses. "You feel better than I could have imagined."

I nod hoping he knows I feel the same way. He squeezes my ass and spreads my cheeks apart. I'm embarrassed that he's probably seeing parts of me no one has inspected so closely before but it all fades away the moment he thrusts into me. I grab onto the edge of the desk to anchor myself and desperately try to hold in the sounds caught in my throat.

"So perfect, Lacy," he whispers. "God, you are

so perfect."

My legs quiver and shake. I've never felt so full. So complete. His cock rubs against places I didn't even know could feel good. His pace picks up and his balls slap at my clit. The popping against my clit coupled with the way he drives into me has me losing control. Fire burns through me and heats my flesh as my nerves explode with pleasure. His breathing gets heavier with each thrust. I'm just wondering if he'll come soon when an intense orgasm seizes me in its clutches. I shudder so hard that if it weren't for the panties in my mouth, I'd probably hear my teeth chattering. The moan I'm desperate to release comes out as a whine as he slams harder into me. A small grunt is the only warning I get before I feel his cock throb inside me. His palms run up and down my ass as he drains out his climax. As soon as we're both sated, he slides out of me.

"Holy…"

I laugh through my panties. He chuckles too and tugs them from my mouth. Instead of giving them back, he pockets them. I'm too worn out to move. I can hear him pulling off the condom and tying it off. It lands with a thud in the trashcan before he pulls his jeans back up and helps me off the desk.

My dress falls back down and the evidence of what we just did in the house of God is gone.

He takes my hands and squeezes them. "You're mine, Lace."

I'm smiling up at him when the door creaks open. Immediately, I bow my head. He starts murmuring a prayer about strength and love. Even after being a very bad boy, he can slip into being one of the good ones at the drop of a hat.

"Amen," he murmurs and releases my hands.

"Amen."

Lucinda clears her throat. "Easton, I'm sorry to interrupt but I had a question about something on the ledger. Before you leave can you clear that up for me?"

"Of course," he says, his voice smooth. As if he wasn't just deep inside of my vagina. "Give us a few more minutes."

Lucinda forces a bright smile and talks through gritted teeth cheerily. "That boy ain't right in the head. I swear he gives me the willies sometimes."

Easton and I both jerk our heads to where she's staring out the window. Bobby stands there holding a rake staring in. I let out a squeak of shock. Easton growls.

"Actually, Lucinda, I'll take a look at the ledger now. Then I'm going to have a chat with Bobby." He gives me an apologetic look. "Can you read some of the highlighted passages in your Bible while I work this out?"

I nod and shoot him a worried look. Will Bobby tell on us? There's no doubt in my mind he got an eyeful just now. Lucinda shuffles out of the office. Before he leaves me to study my Bible, he steals a quick kiss on my lips and then stalks away.

SEVEN

EASTON

I DON'T WANT TO HAVE TO FIRE THE KID. I TRULY don't. But he needs to cut the stalker crap out. When I'd seen him earlier with Lacy pinned against the church doors, I'd been prepared to rip him from her and beat his ass. Luckily, he was just invading her space. He didn't touch her.

Yet.

Irritation bubbles up inside me.

Bobby is a wild card. Anyone with brain damage is. They're no longer wired like the rest of us. I've seen Bobby act impulsively and say strange things. Plenty of times, I've seen him gawk at girls in the congregation. It never bothered me before.

Until now.

Now he's looking at what's mine. And dammit, she is mine. It was reckless and irresponsible to screw her at church but I did it and I don't regret it. Well, not the sex part. Shame niggles at me that I chose to have sex with her so disrespectfully in God's house. I'm dying to get her back to my place where we don't have to rush or fear getting caught. And where I don't have a picture of Jesus in my office staring down at me, reminding me what a sinner I am. We certainly don't have to worry about creepy voyeurs.

I stalk outside and find Bobby raking some leaves as if he wasn't just watching me pound into a teenager. His bright red cheeks give him away. With a groan, I walk over to him.

"Hey, Bobby," I grunt. "Can I talk to you for a minute?"

He nods but doesn't make eye contact with me.

"I want to apologize for what you saw. That was meant to be private and I'm sorry you had to see that," I mutter.

He lifts his chin and a flicker of anger flashes in his normally gentle eyes. "Lashey is pwetty. I wuv Lashey."

I clench my jaw. "Lacy is very pretty but she's mine," I clip out, my voice hard. "I don't want you cornering her anymore or watching her when she thinks she's alone. Understand?"

"I want Lashey too." His brows furrow together making the long scar on his forehead wrinkle.

I step closer to him and glower. "You can't have her, buddy. I'm sorry."

"I take her next time."

My blood runs cold and I grip him by both shoulders. "Do you like this job?"

He nods.

"Well, if you want to keep it, then I need for you to back the hell off Lacy. Are we clear? Your comments and actions are bordering on grounds for termination."

His nostrils flare. "But—"

"Do I need to call your pa?"

He widens his eyes. "No, don't call Pa."

"Okay, then. It's settled. No more standing around peeking in windows or following pretty girls. You clean the church and take care of the grounds. Then you go home. That's it. Are we clear, buddy?"

Defeated, he nods. "You wuv her, Pashtor?"

My chest thunders and I tell him the truth. "I'm

getting there faster than I'd like to admit. Now, get back to work."

I ruffle his sweaty head and he snort laughs. I think we've sorted out that problem but only time will tell.

"I'm taking Lacy home," I announce to Lucinda once we've settled the books. She's deep in concentration so she waves us off. Bobby has long since left, thank God, and now I'm practically dying to get Lacy home with me. When she approaches my motorcycle outside, she frowns.

"I have to ride on this thing with no underwear in a dress?" Her golden eyebrow is arched and her lip curls up.

I laugh and hand her the helmet. "I'm not letting anyone but me see what's under that dress. Got it, vixen?"

Once she has the helmet on her head and is straddled behind me, I take off. She hugs me tight and it drives me mental knowing her bare pussy is pressed against my ass. By the time we reach my house, I'm sporting a hard-on bigger than Dallas. As much as I want to push my dick inside her again, we slip into our normal Saturday routine.

Television.

Talk about everything under the sun.

Nap and then pizza.

More television.

"How do you feel?" I ask her, my voice low and raspy.

She lifts up from where she's cuddled against my side. "I feel fine. Why?"

Running my fingers up along her hips, I murmur, "I meant between your legs."

Her cheeks redden and she bites on her bottom lip. "Oh. There. It feels like it might need some attention."

I laugh and stroke a strand of blonde hair from her eyes. "Is that so? With my tongue? My fingers? My cock?"

She swallows. "Maybe all three."

"Well, we better go take a look. We're wasting daylight."

A squeal escapes her when I rise from the couch, taking her with me. I carry her down the hallway to my room. Once inside, I set her on the bed and peel away her dress. I love looking at her perfect honey-colored skin. She tastes sweet too.

With my eyes searing into hers, I begin popping through buttons as quickly as I can. I shed the dress shirt and then tug off the undershirt. Her eyes widen upon seeing my chest.

"Wow…" she breathes in appreciation.

"What?"

"That chest. I mean…" she trails off her and her eyes drop to my lower abs. "I didn't realize you were inked everywhere. You mean to tell me the good boy preacher was hiding all this underneath his clothes?"

I shrug as I pop the button on my jeans. "I'm not inked *everywhere*."

She licks her lips which makes my cock jolt in my pants. "Prove it."

With my eyes glued to her pretty mouth, I unzip my jeans and let them fall to the floor. When I hook my thumbs into the waistband of my black boxers, she bites on her plump pink lip. I push the material down my thighs and revel in the whine that escapes her. Her blue eyes are flickering with lust the moment my thick cock bobs out. I reach for a condom on the nightstand and tear the foil before sheathing myself with the rubber.

"You're not tattooed there," she observes.

"You're not tattooed anywhere."

Her eyes that were flaming with desire dim suddenly and she looks away. The emotion is so brief that if I didn't pay attention to every blink, every breath she takes, I'd have missed it. I pounce on her and lay her back with my body covering hers. My cock aches pressed against her but my heart aches more.

I want to know every time she's sad. Just like I want to know each time she's happy.

"What is it?" I murmur, my mouth pressing soft kisses along her jawline to her ear. "Where'd you go just then?"

She lets out a heavy sigh. "I can't get anything past you." Her voice is almost ashamed. "It's nothing."

I suck on her earlobe and then breathe against her ear. "It was something. Tell me, Lace. Tell me everything."

Her fingers slide up my shoulders and up my neck to my hair. I love when she clings to me as though she'll die if I were to leave. I'm not going anywhere.

"I want one but you'll probably think it's stupid," she whispers.

I spread her thighs apart and settle my body against hers. I grip her jaw and stare down at her. "I never think you're stupid, honey. You're the smartest girl I know."

She laughs and then her blue eyes meet mine, her brows pinched together. "I want to get one. A pair of angel wings to signify the angel I lost."

I kiss her mouth. "I don't think that's stupid at all. In fact, I'll take you to get it done on your birthday."

"Really?"

"Really." I nip at her bottom lip. "Now stop holding things in around me. Let them out and let me carry your burdens with you."

She whimpers when I start rubbing against her. My cock slides up between the lips of her pussy teasing her.

"Easton…"

"Yeah, baby?"

"I need you."

"Like this?" I push into her with one hard thrust that has her screaming. I love her screams. Now that I've had one, I want to pull many, many more from her.

"Yes," she moans. "Just like that."

Our mouths crash together as I piston against her. Her heels dig into my ass and her fingernails claw the hell out of my shoulders. Being inside of her is the best feeling I've had in my entire life. Nothing else matters but her. Her body is tight and responsive. Mine.

"Fuck," I hiss against her mouth. "Holy fuck."

She giggles and I take the opportunity to strike at her neck with my teeth. I bite at the flesh and groan when her pussy clenches around me each time I do it. My sweet girl likes it a little rough. I suck on the flesh before biting hard enough to make her beg me to stop.

I won't stop.

I can't stop.

All I can do is devour her. Every decadent inch. I give her a reprieve from the biting and suckle her earlobe as I drive brutally into her. It's been so long since I've touched a woman that being with Lacy feels like heaven. It goes against everything I've been taught in The Bible but I can't seem to care. She's innocent and perfect—being with her is like being with an angel. It can't be wrong because it feels too right.

Her breathing is sharp and uneven. I don't know if she's close to coming but I want her unraveling beneath me when I get ready to climax. I slide my hand between us and massage her hot clit. Each time I slide in and out of her, my fingertips brush along my dick. Her moans get louder until she's right on the cusp. She seems to hold her breath and go silent for a beat before she jolts beneath me. My eyes snap shut as my nuts seize up with my orgasm. I throb out my release with a string of curse words tumbling from my lips. When I finally collapse on her, she starts giggling again.

"Your mouth gets dirty in the heat of the moment."

I growl. "When I'm inside you, I lose my mind."

She hugs me and kisses my sweaty hair. "Good. The feeling is mutual. Now when can I clean my dirty preacher boy up?"

I grope her tit and lift up to grin at her. "Don't let the water and soap fool you. I can defile you just as easily in there."

Pulling away from her, I tug off the used condom and dispose of it. Once the water is turned on, I saunter back out to find her sitting on the edge of the bed looking like a picture of innocence. Her golden waves hang in front of her tits hiding them from me and her legs are primly crossed at the ankle. She wears an expression that alludes to the exact opposite of getting drilled in her tight pussy by her preacher who's old enough to be her father.

"Come here, honey," I growl as I snag her wrist.

She's all smiles as I pull her to her feet. Her arms encircle the back of my neck and she stares up at me with such a strong emotion that I'm nearly knocked over by it. I slide my hands to her ass and lift her. She hooks her silky legs around my waist. Having her open and ready again has my eager cock waking right up. It bobs against her ass as I walk with her to the shower. As soon as I step under the spray and jerk the curtain closed, our mouths fuse together. I can't seem to get enough of her and it's as though the feeling is mutual on her end. Our tongues slide against each other in a desperate way.

"You're mine," I murmur against her mouth as the hot water rains down on us. I don't know why I feel the urge to state this so often but it's truth. She's mine and nothing will come between us. I won't let it, dammit.

"Yes," she agrees. "Yours."

I squeeze her ass to pull her away from me and then I push my thickness deep inside her with one hard thrust. She squeals into my mouth but then she gets on the same page as me and her body rocks against mine. I pin her to the cold tile wall for leverage so I can drive harder into her. Over and over again, I hammer into her because she's mine.

"Easton!" she cries out. "Oh, God!"

We're a tangled mess of wet limbs and bumping teeth. The slapping of our flesh and our feral sounds creates a song I could listen to on repeat. I keep her upright between the wall and my one hand on her ass but use my free hand to massage her sensitive clit. She whimpers and begs and then she's coming. Hard and without a care in the world. Her head tilts back and she wails, baring her beautiful throat to me. I latch onto her creamy neck and then I'm coming too.

Thrust.

Thrust.

Thrust.

And then, dammit, I'm pulling out and spending the rest of my climax against her taut stomach between us. Neither of us say a word. She just clutches onto me tightly and buries her face against my neck. I pull her from the wall when she shivers and back under the hot spray where I simply hold her until the water runs cold.

EIGHT

Lacy

It's been three and a half weeks since Easton and I started sleeping together. Of course we keep it a secret. The last thing we need is for him to go to prison for sleeping with me when my birthday is just a month away. It doesn't stop him though from feeling me up in his office and claiming me on his desk every Saturday with Lucinda on the other side of the door. He did, however, hang a curtain in his office so that Bobby wouldn't get any more free shows.

I shudder at the thought of Bobby watching us.

"Are you cold, sweetheart?" Mom asks.

She's all smiles and relaxed now that Aunt Kimmie is back on her feet and on her own. It's just us having girl time once again. We're at a nail salon with our feet soaking before we get pedicures.

"I'm fine. Where are we going to eat after this?"

"Moon Wok is around the corner. Want Chinese?" she asks.

I give her a smile and nod.

"Did you send off any of those college applications?" she asks absently as she digs in her purse.

"Mmmhmmm," I lie and thankfully she's too distracted to notice. I graduated from high school last weekend and she's been more adamant about my getting a business degree like her. I've been told a million times that I'll have an internship position there while I go to school. Problem is, I'm not sure if that's what I want to do. I've never been a numbers person like my friend Ava Prince. I'm more of a creative type. But, according to Mom and the world, you can't pay the bills with creativity.

My phone buzzes in my pocket and I quickly retrieve it.

Preach: I miss you, vixen.

My smile widens. Now that school has officially ended, we're hoping to see more of each other than just Saturdays which was our only real day to be together. Mom would drop me off in the morning and he didn't take me back home until much later that evening. We'd spend the entire day together. *The Walking Dead*. Pizza. And as much sex as we could squeeze in until I'd have to cry uncle when my vagina was worn out and we'd give in to heavy petting instead. His cock is brutal. A weapon. Sometimes, I can only handle so much before I'm walking bowlegged and sore for days.

Me: I miss you too.

Preach: When can I see you again?

Me: Soon. Now that summer is officially here, I can come hang out with you at the church. Maybe help you work.

Preach: If you come to the church, I can assure you, I won't get any work done. But I do love the idea of seeing you every day.

Me: You make me happy.

I let out a sigh and Mom laughs beside me.

"Okay, Lacy Lou. You're going to have to spill," she says in amusement. "You've practically got hearts in your eyes."

I freeze and tuck my phone away in my purse. "It's nothing."

"Bryce? The boy from church?"

I cringe because I don't want to lie to her. She's been coming every Sunday with me so surely she's noticed that I don't talk to Bryce much. Only in passing. Besides, anytime Bryce comes at me, Lydia plays interference. I'm not as intimidated by her now and it shocks me that she seems to want to protect me from Bryce, especially when it feels like his brother Bobby is the bigger threat.

"Uh, not exactly."

Her blue eyes twinkle in anticipation. We've always been close and I'm not one to withhold information from her. Guilt gnaws at me. I want to tell her but then I worry about how that could affect Easton if she reacts badly.

"Baby," she coos. "You went from elated to positively frightened. Whatever it is, you can tell me. I'm not going to be upset. We've been through a lot together. I think we can handle whatever it is."

I swallow down my emotion. I'm afraid she won't understand our relationship. Telling her in the middle of the salon seems like a terrible idea.

"Can I tell you over dinner?

Her brows furrow in concern. "Sweetheart, you're scaring me."

My tears spill over and I wring my hands together. She reaches over and tugs my hand into hers. When I glance at her, she's crying too. The women who are working on our feet chatter on in a language I don't understand but don't ask what's wrong.

"Mom, I'm in love," I choke out. "Not infatuation like before. Real love. The kind of love that is so deep it hurts. He's good to me. Sweet and giving. Listens to me when I'm upset. I've told him everything about me and he still sticks around."

A flash of anger glimmers in her blue eyes. She knows. How could she not? I stare at him every Sunday as he preaches the gospel. With hearts in my eyes as she says.

"I know you're angry and I'm so sorry. I wasn't seeking it out. I'm not some magnet for older men. He isn't a pervert. We're good together." An ugly sob rips from me and she squeezes my hand. "Mom, please don't be upset with me. Please."

A worker rushes over to us and offers a box of tissues. I hold it out to my mother so she can take some and then I set the box in my lap. Both of us dab at our tears.

"I learned a lot after Sean. I'd learned what it felt like to be used. To be someone's plaything. The consequences gave me Mikey. And then Mikey died. I was so devastated. It forced me to grow up. I watch the girls at school every day and I'm not like them. I feel like I aged ten years after the Sean fiasco…"

"You named the baby?"

Hot tears roll down my cheeks and I nod. I realize I kept this, along with many other sad parts of me locked tight inside me. Easton is the only one who knows everything.

"Oh, baby," she cries out as she kisses my hand. "I'm so sorry. I knew you were upset but I had no idea you named him. That you still carried all that grief. I thought you were still hung up on Sean."

"Sean was a jerk," I say, shaking my head. "It's Mikey who breaks my heart every day. And then…"

"Easton," we both say in unison.

"Please don't be mad," I beg.

Her frown mars her pretty face. "He should know better."

"I'm not an itch to be scratched or some midlife crisis, Mom. We have a connection. From the very get-go. He peels apart my layers and finds the real me." I sniffle and blow my nose. "I'm happy. He helped me find my happiness."

My mother smiles, the stormy expression still

swirling in her blue eyes. “I know. I knew something had brought my little girl back to me. I thought it was the church. I didn’t realize it was the preacher. The signs were there…” she trails off. “I don’t know what to do. You’re so young. He’s…He’s…”

“Almost forty. I know. I’ll be legal soon though. And, Mom, you don’t have to *do* anything. When we’re together, age isn’t even an issue. We’re happy.” I plead with my eyes. “I’ve made some pretty bad judgment calls this past year but you have to trust me. Easton is the real deal.”

Her lips purse together. “Invite him to dinner.”

I gape at her. “W-What? Why?”

“If he’s special to you and you love him, I deserve to ask him some questions about his intentions. It’s the only way I can accept this. I need to see for myself,” she says, her tone serious.

“Okay…” I pull out my phone and smile at the last text he left me while I was talking to Mom.

Preach: You make me happier.

Me: Can you meet me at Moon Wok for dinner?

Preach: I’d love to. Might have to figure out a way to ditch my friend though.

Me: Bring your friend…Mom knows.

The three dots move and then stop. Then move again.

Preach: Everything's going to be okay, Lace. I promise.

Tears well in my eyes.

Me: I think it will be.

Mom is quiet for the rest of the pedicure. I can tell she's deep in thought which scares me a little. But she's not yelling which is a plus. We arrive at Moon Wok and she starts inside. Someone grabs my elbow and drags me away from the door. I spin around in shock.

"I thought that was you."

I freeze in horror. How did he get out of prison? My knees buckle and Sean Polk catches me before I hit the pavement. He looks the same. Styled blonde hair. Crisp polo shirt and khakis. Fancy and smug.

I'm going to be sick.

"Lacy," he murmurs, his voice like nails on a chalkboard. All it does is remind me of Mikey. My loss. I don't miss Sean at all. He used me and I hate him.

"Let me go," I choke out.

His grip tightens.

"Lacy!" my mom cries out my name and then

she's rushing over to us. She shoves at him but his grip on my bicep is too tight for her to wrench us apart.

Heavy footsteps stomp up behind me and then a tattooed arm reaches past me to snag Sean by his throat. It shocks him enough that he lets me go. Easton continues storming away with Sean in his grip until he slams him up against the wall.

"You. Are. Not. Allowed. To. Touch. Her," he seethes, his shoulders heaving with rage.

"Easton, man," a familiar voice bellows. "Let him go. Now."

Mom wraps me up in a hug and shoots daggers with her eyes at Sean. With a growl, Easton releases Sean and takes a step back.

"Leave," he snarls. "Now."

Sean steals one more glance at me before he storms off down the sidewalk away from us. As soon as he's gone, Easton turns and all but plucks me from my mom's arms.

"Are you okay? Did he hurt you?" His body ripples with fury.

"Why is he out of jail?" I cry out.

Mr. Alexander, our attorney—I still haven't figured out why he's here—grumbles. "I'm about to find out." And then he's on the phone stalking away.

Easton pulls away to search my face with concerned eyes. "I won't let him touch you. You're safe." His mouth presses to mine and he kisses me possessively until my mom clears her throat.

We both tense.

In the heat of the moment, we sort of lost ourselves.

He jerks away and spears his fingers through his hair messing it up. Then he juts out his hand to shake Mom's. She takes his hand but scowls.

"We should head inside," she tells us both, her tone icy.

Easton shoots me an apologetic stare but I shake it off. He has nothing to be sorry about. Mom has made it this far without blowing a gasket, we'll make it through to the end. Boldly, he takes my hand and squeezes it. It feels weird being open about our relationship in public but I love it. Mom doesn't even argue when Easton slides into the booth beside me and wraps his strong arm around me. We're quiet until our attorney shows up and plops down beside Mom.

"This is my buddy Dane," Easton introduces. "Dane this is—"

"Stephanie and Lacy Greenwood. My clients. Yes, I know them," Dane says in a dry tone.

Easton frowns and Mom shrugs.

"It's a small town, that's for sure," she says with a sigh.

Dane's gaze skims over the way Easton has a hold on me and his face falls. "No way, man. This girl you've been going on and on about is little Lacy Greenwood?" He scrubs his face and shakes his head. "Why?"

Easton growls. "Do you think I purposefully went and sought out something illegal that could not only get me fired but sent to prison again?"

Dane slaps the table. "Don't say another word. Those words can be used against you," he warns. "And, goddammit, I feel like there's a huge conflict of interest for me now. I'm not sure I can be your attorney anymore."

Mom laughs and it's harsh. "Cut the crap, Dane. You're talking out of your ass again." Easton snorts when Dane appears to have his feelings hurt but then Mom shoots her glare at him. "Now my primary focus is not Pastor McAvoy's future. My focus is on why the hell that bastard is out of prison and attacking my daughter!" Her eyes find mine and the love in her gaze warms my heart. Mom has always had my back one hundred percent.

Dane clears his throat. “Huge problem. Sean is out on a technicality. Since the Feds were brought on because of the severity of the case, our local PD wasn’t involved much. Turns out, the Fed leading the entire operation was just busted for tampering with evidence on multiple cases. Polk’s attorneys took that and ran with it. Made claims that testimonies were falsified and evidence was mishandled. Claimed that the entire case didn’t have a leg to stand on because the one handling it was guilty of crimes that may have altered the way the case was dealt with. They appealed and fucking won. Those bastards moved quickly and quietly.” He scrubs at his jaw and frowns. “I’m so sorry. I didn’t know he was out.”

Mom sighs. “It’s done. But I want to file a restraining order against him.”

“I’ll call Sheriff,” Easton says. He kisses my temple before sliding out of the booth and walking off.

Dane frowns at me. “I didn’t realize one of my best friends was dating my client. I’m sorry, ladies.”

“Dating. Is that what we’re calling it?” Mom asks, her blonde brow arched at me.

"Mom." My cheeks blaze red when Easton returns to his seat.

"The sheriff will get on his ass," Easton says, unknowingly changing the subject. "Polk won't step within five hundred feet of Lacy."

Mom stares at him with narrowed eyes before letting out a huff. "Okay, so now that Polk is out of the way, I want to know what your intentions are with my daughter. If this is some sort of fling that ends when you get bored—"

"I won't get bored," Easton bites out. "Stephanie, I love her." My heart thuds in my chest. He turns and presses a kiss to my cheek. "Lacy, I love you." His words to me are murmured just low enough for me to hear. His hand clasps mine and he squeezes.

Mom sighs. "So I guess this whole counseling thing was my fault? I've been dropping you off for months thinking you were actually getting help."

I shake my head at her. "Mom, we *do* talk. He's helped me a lot. I'm more at peace than I ever was."

"Did she show you the book?" Easton asks Mom.

I shoot him an embarrassed look but his gaze is on my mother.

"What book?"

"Easton," Dane warns.

Mom nudges him. "What book, Easton? Like a sex book?"

"Mom!" I screech.

A nervous looking employee approaches our table where we're making a racket and points at the buffet. "Moon Wok is self-serve. Plates are there."

We all chuckle and nod. Once the lady leaves, Easton turns his attention back to Mom. "The book about Mikey."

Mom's face crumples and she reaches across the table to hold my hand. "What book, sweetheart?"

I'm embarrassed but I shouldn't be. I'm proud of what Mikey could have become. I'm not ashamed of him. "I've been writing a fictional story about Mikey grown into a rambunctious little boy and his mother who loves him with everything."

Tears well in Mom's eyes and she glances at Easton. "You've read it?"

"I have," he confirms. "And it's good. She's got talent."

I beam at him through my tears. "Thank you."

"I also know that she doesn't want to go to college for business. She wants to explore her writing."

He winks at me.

"You didn't tell me this," Mom murmurs, hurt lacing her tone. "I've been pressuring you about college and you never spoke up. Oh, Lacy."

I give her a warm smile. "I was going to bring it up at the right time. You seemed so excited. I didn't want to burst your bubble."

Mom glances back and forth between Easton and I. "Sweetheart, we'll talk more about your future later. I want you to talk to me always though. Even if you're afraid of disappointing me." She smiles and her eyes brighten. "You've always been my greatest achievement."

Dane smirks and slaps the table. "Well, as fun and mushy as this was, I'm headed out. You ladies want to run this knucklehead home after you eat since he and I rode together?"

Mom gives Dane's elbow a squeeze. "Of course. Keep me posted on the Polk situation."

"Don't forget to swing by the station later and file your report against Sean," he instructs as he slides out of the booth. "I think everything will work out just how it's supposed to."

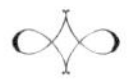

It's been over a week since we ran into Sean and my relationship with Easton blew up with my mom. Thankfully, she didn't freak out too much. Just lectured me about safe sex. I showed her my book I was writing about Mikey. This morning, before she dropped me off, she gave me a new laptop for my graduation gift so I can type my story out. We both cried ugly tears.

"Almost done?" Easton chirps from the doorway of his office. Lucinda and Bobby have long gone home for the day.

I stretch my arms above my head and bask in the way his gaze skims over my cleavage in my dress. "I'm done. I was just double checking the totals."

He strides in looking good enough to eat this Saturday afternoon in a pair of dark jeans and fitted white T-shirt. Since he didn't have anyone to see but me, he didn't dress up. And that's fine by me. I get to see more of his tattoos and all his sculpted glory.

I stand from the desk to meet his embrace. Even though Mom knows, we've still kept our relationship from others. I'm underage according to the law and he has an image to uphold here at the church. I'd asked him if Lucinda knows but he doesn't think she does.

"Come on," he tells me when he pulls away from our hug. His gaze is hot as he stares intently at me. "I want to do something in the sanctuary."

He clasps my hand and leads me out of the office to the sanctuary. We walk down the aisle to the front where Mom and I always sit in the first pew.

"Sit." He pats the top of the backside of the pew. "There."

I lift a brow but obey. "What are we doing?"

His grin is wicked. "Each other."

"Easton!"

He shrugs. "I turned off the security cameras. Just you and me."

I point behind him to the crucifix on the wall. "And Jesus."

With a smirk, he peels off his shirt and bares his colorful chest to me. "Jesus says to love one another."

"Jesus didn't mean literally love her body inside the church," I counter with a laugh.

But then he's on his knees on the pew seat and spreading my thighs apart. I yelp when he rips my panties rather than him pulling them down my thighs.

"I don't like your panties," he says with a grunt. Smug ass.

I'm miffed for all of three seconds because then he's burying his nose against my clit as he spears my sex with his tongue. Dear God, he's good with that part of his body. My eyes roll back as he devours me with the hunger of a hundred men. I'm gripping the back of the pew so hard I'm afraid if I relax just a fraction, I'll fall backward with a crash. The intensity at which he eats me out has me losing my mind quickly. I come fast and hard, shrieking his name in pleasure.

"Dress. Off. Now." His eyes have turned their darker shade of mostly blue—the way he gets when he's hung up his preacher robe and turned into the demon dead set on ravishing my body.

I tug at the ties of my halter dress exposing my bare breasts to him. He slips a condom from his pocket and hands it to me to tear open. Once his pants and boxers have been pushed down his thighs, I take his massive cock in my hands and roll the condom slowly onto his throbbing shaft. Blazing blue-green eyes watch my every movement. I take satisfaction in the way his breathing has become ragged and uneven. The moment the condom is fully on, he grips my hips as he guides himself into me.

"That's it," he coos, his cock pushing in at an

agonizingly slow pace. "Take all of it, vixen. This is yours."

I grab onto his shoulders and tilt my head back so that my hair hangs down my back. His fingers massage my clit that's still slippery from his mouth as he starts thrusting brutally into me. I love when his eyes turn mostly blue and have a manic, uncontrolled quality in them. He forgets everything when around me. I'm his sole focus. And truth be told, he's mine.

It feels dirty having sex on the pew I normally sit on each week beside my mom but I like it. Seeing Easton so out of control is enough to have me drawing closer to orgasm rather quickly.

"God, I love you, Lace," he grunts, his movements becoming shaky. He grabs my hips and pulls me off the back of the pew so that he impales me with his cock. All I can do is hold on for the ride as he maneuvers my hips so that I'm fucking him. I cry out when my orgasm hits suddenly. My fingernails pierce his flesh as the trembling begins. He makes a feral hissing sound and then his cock is throbbing inside of me with his release. We're still a tangled mess of sweaty limbs when we hear a voice.

"My Lashey!" Bobby shouts.

Easton's eyes are wide with horror as he stares behind me. I crane my neck and my stomach bottoms out to see Bobby, his brother Bryce, and who I know are their parents.

"Pastor McAvoy," the woman chokes out. "What on earth?"

"Meet me in my office," Easton booms.

I cringe at his tone and glance back at him. His face is beet red. Shame glimmers in his eyes but what's worse is the terror. The door creaks shut and he jerks out of me. Once he sets me down on the seat of the pew, he yanks off the condom and quickly ties it up. I'm still sitting there half-naked and in shock when his hard voice startles me.

"Please get dressed and call your mom to come get you. This may take a while," he grits out, his palm scrubbing over his handsome face. The panic washing over his features jolts me into action. I quickly tie up the dress, snatch up my ruined panties and used condom, and scurry after him up the aisle.

He makes a beeline into his office and then comes back holding my purse. His brows are crushed together. I hate that he's upset. I wish I knew what to do but something tells me being around him will be worse.

"I love you. Everything is going to be okay," I assure him and press a chaste kiss to his mouth that still smells like me. I stuff my panties into my purse and toss the condom in the nearest trashcan. "Call me later."

He stares at me for a beat longer and then nods before stalking into the office. The door closes behind him. With hot tears in my eyes, I quickly text my mom.

Me: OMG, Mom. Something bad has happened. Can you come get me from the church?

She responds immediately.

Mom: What's wrong? Did he hurt you?

I swipe away my tears and text back.

Me: No. He's good to me. We were caught being indecent by some people who go to church here.

Mom: Oh, Lacy.

Me: I don't want him to go to prison!

Mom: I'm getting in the car now. I'll be there within ten minutes. We'll talk then. Love you, Lacy Lou.

Me: Love you too.

I hurry outside to wait for her. The Johnston's SUV sits beside Easton's motorcycle. I'm irrationally angry at them. Why did they even come here? If it weren't for Bobby using his key to let them in, we'd never have been caught. It was supposed to be safe.

It makes me worry for Easton. I'm still not legal and if they take this to the police, I'm afraid of what they'll do to him. He can't go back to prison because of me. I won't let that happen.

And to make matters worse…

How does this impact his job?

I'm crying hot tears when the door opens. Bobby and Bryce walk outside alone.

"They're still talking. They wanted to talk to Pastor McAvoy alone," Bryce tells me, his tone cold.

I keep my gaze on the concrete. "Okay."

"My Lashey," Bobby grumbles.

I shoot him a scathing glare. "I am not yours! Stop saying that!"

Bryce snaps at me. "Don't talk to him that way!"

Jerking my gaze to his, I'm startled at his threatening stance. His hands are fisted and his nostrils are flaring with fury. Unease creeps up my spine.

"Just leave me alone," I utter as I start walking along the side of the building to get away from them. I'm almost to the corner when I hear heavy footsteps running. I let out a squeak and manage to round the corner before someone is pressing their body against mine, pinning me to the brick wall. My purse hits the floor with a thud.

"Lashey, don't wun," Bobby says, his chest heaving with exertion. I can feel his erection pressed into my hip.

I let out a shriek and push at him but he goes nowhere. I manage to wiggle to the side but then Bryce is right in front of me. He snags my wrists and pins them roughly to the brick wall.

"Be nice to my brother," he snarls, slamming my pinned arms against the wall. My knuckles burn from being scraped.

"Let go of me you freak," I snap at Bryce before spitting at him.

He growls but doesn't let go. His eyes flicker with meanness. "Better hurry and get a taste, Bobby, before it's too late."

I let out a blood-curdling scream when Bobby nears me. His grip is powerful as his fingers bite into my jaw. He forcefully turns my head to face his.

"Lashey pwetty," he says, a bright smile on his face. And then he presses his mouth to mine.

I thrash and squirm but Bryce is stronger than me. At one point he pushes his knee painfully against my sex to keep me from moving. Tears roll out continuously as Bobby tries to stick his tongue inside my mouth. Bryce urges him on telling him he deserves me.

"She's just a whore, like in The Bible. Whores belong to everyone," Bryce tells Bobby.

"Whore. Lashey a whore," Bobby says excitedly.

I sob and wish I was stronger. When Bobby roughly grips my breast through my dress, I choke out my tears. But when he slides his hand lower, I begin to check out mentally. Bryce's heavy breathing and laughing is something that will haunt me for a long time. And Bobby's fingers aren't gentle as he finds my bare sex under my dress. He shoves a finger brutally inside of me causing me to wail. I begin to black out, my mind prepared to protect me from the abuse when I hear a wild screech.

Items clatter to the ground as someone hits Bryce with something. I'm dazed and confused about what's happening. Bryce stumbles away from me and even Bobby lets go. Then the savior is at my side screaming at them as she sprays something out in front of her. The guys both start choking and yelling but she's already dragging me around the building.

"My Lacy Lou," Mom sobs as she drags me toward the car.

I'm shuddering and sobbing so hard it takes everything in her to keep me upright. She manages to get me inside the car and get the engine started.

"I-I lost everything in my purse when I hit that motherfucker with it. I d-don't want to go back for it right now. I n-need to get you to the station," she chatters through her tears as she tears out of the parking lot.

I don't have my phone. She doesn't have hers. We're a mess. But my mom saved me. She rescued me.

When she reaches for my hand, I clutch it desperately. My voice is raw from screaming. "Mommy," is all I can manage.

NINE

EASTON

JAY AND JENNIFER JOHNSTON HAVE BEEN A PART of my church since the very beginning when I began preaching. Each week, they supported me and brought their friends. When Bobby had the accident, I'd gone to the hospital and prayed with them. And when he was better, but certainly not all there, I offered him a job at the church.

I'm close with this family.

Which is what makes it incredibly awkward that they walked in on me having sex with Lacy. Shame burns through me. I'm not sorry for being with Lacy, but I am sorry for what their family witnessed.

Neither one of them can look me in the eye as they sit across from my desk. They've long since sent their sons away so we could discuss what happened.

"For what it's worth, I'm sorry," I say, my voice soft. "I can't even begin to tell you how ashamed and embarrassed I am."

Jennifer's face burns bright. Jay has taken to nervously clicking a pen he'd snagged from my desk.

"I know what I've done should be grounds for termination as pastor here at the church. I'm not sure where we go from here but I know it's going to be a long road. My only request is that you keep Miss Greenwood out of it as much as possible. She doesn't deserve it. I'm the adult here and I knew better." My jaw clenches and I wish I could rewind. I'm such an idiot. Not only did I get busted, but what I did was disrespectful to God. I am disgusted with myself.

"Isn't that the girl who was caught up with Sean Polk?" Jennifer asks. Her eyes lift to mine and a flicker of anger shimmers in her blue eyes. "If my memory serves me right, she's not even of age yet."

I swallow and scrub at my face with my palm. "Not quite."

Jay's narrowed eyes find mine. "That's a crime, Pastor."

My anxiety is starting to skyrocket because I don't like where this conversation is going. I wish my dad were here to help guide me through this. I should have called him and Mom first.

"I'm sorry. My actions were reprehensible," I admit. My phone starts buzzing but I ignore it for now. "After I leave here, I'll go down to the station and tell Sheriff McMahon what I did. I promise you that. As far as my job here goes, can you at least let me talk to my father before you do or say anything to anyone?"

Jennifer presses her lips together and her nose turns pink. "I don't know. This is huge, Pastor. You've committed a crime with an underage girl. My children had to witness it. *We* had to witness it. I'm disturbed and think you should step down at once."

Jay reaches over and squeezes her hand in support. "I agree. You should make arrangements to have someone fill in tomorrow until we can get this mess sorted out. I'll be the first to admit, you've disappointed me, Easton. Incredibly so."

I hang my head shamefully and glance at my phone. Mom is blowing up my texts.

Mom: Call me.

Mom: EASTON CALL ME ASAP.

Mom: Meet me down at the police station.

Something awful has happened.

More guilt floods through me. She knows about what Lacy and I did. How? I have no idea. I'm about to open my mouth when we hear a commotion in the hall. My door bursts open and both Bobby and Bryce stagger in crying. Tears stream from their eyes and they keep rubbing at them.

"What on earth is happening?" Jennifer shouts as she stands to go to her boys.

"Lashey's mom huwt me!" Bobby cries out.

"She sprayed us with mace!" Bryce exclaims.

I'm on my feet in an instant. "What happened?" I demand.

When neither of them pipe up, I get a bad feeling.

"We'll talk more about this tomorrow. Something has come up with my mother. I'm going to have to leave and head to the police station. Bobby has the key so he can lock up. I'm sorry but I have to go," I blurt out as I snag my helmet and keys.

Jennifer is fussing over the boys but I don't have time to sort out what happened. All I know is something has my mom frantic. It takes all of ten minutes to get to the station. When I see Mom's Honda Pilot and Stephanie Greenwood's Nissan Maxima, the bad feeling turns into one of dread.

Here it is.

The moment where everything comes out and they put me back in cuffs.

My life is over.

At least I was happy with Lacy for a little while. Being with her was worth it.

I cut off the engine and stride into the building with my helmet under my arm. As soon as I enter the lobby area, I'm shocked to find Lacy sobbing with both my mom and hers hugging her. Dad shoots me a sad look.

"Lacy," I bark out as I rush over to her. Mom takes my helmet and then I'm embracing my girl. "What's wrong?"

"T-They h-hurt me," Lacy chatters out and then shudders.

Confusion melts away as my blood begins to boil. One quick look at Stephanie and the furious glare on her face is enough to know that Bobby and Bryce were to blame. The mace should have been my first clue.

"I'm going to kill them," I snarl.

Dad grips my shoulder from behind. "No, you're not. Take a walk with me, son."

I press a kiss to Lacy's hot, wet cheek. "I'll be right back, honey. I promise."

She nods and then I'm stalking from the lobby to the only interrogation room this police station has. Once inside, I find Sheriff McMahon and Deputy Gentry Adair looking somber.

"You have to arrest them," I bark out. "Tell me what happened and then go arrest them before I kill them."

Sheriff shakes his head. "We'll get to that. Have a seat, Easton."

"I'd rather stand." My entire body ripples with rage. Once again, Dad gives me his support by clutching my shoulder.

"I know what happened," Sheriff says. "I don't have to tell you what sort of problems this presents for you being that you're having sex with a minor."

"Don't admit to anything," Dad mutters from behind me. "Dane's on his way."

I grit my teeth. "What. Did. They. Do. To. Her?"

Sheriff frowns. "They sexually assaulted her according to Miss Greenwood. Her mother thwarted the assault and brought her straight here."

A roar rips from me. They did that while I was sitting in my damn office with their parents. I didn't protect her. I should have known better. When I start to turn around, Dad blocks me.

"Move," I snarl.

"No. You're not going to get yourself thrown in prison again. I won't let you," Dad bites back.

"Now, before you showed up a few minutes ago," Sheriff says, "I got a call from Jennifer Johnston claiming that you were having sex with Miss Greenwood when they arrived. And then, she said her boys were assaulted by Mrs. Greenwood. So basically right now we have their word against yours and the Greenwoods."

"We'll just pull up the security footage and…" I trail off and curse. "I turned it off."

Sheriff nods. "And as your friend, that may keep you out of prison. We have no proof that you had sex with Miss Greenwood because she denies it. Just that the Johnston's say you did. On the other side of the coin, we don't have any recordings showing them assaulting her. If she goes to the hospital and they perform a rape kit, they're going to find more than Bobby's DNA. Right now, she's refusing to go to the hospital."

I close my eyes and let out a ragged breath. "So what do we do?"

The door swings open and Dane strides in. "You let your attorney handle it. Boys, I'll need a minute with my client."

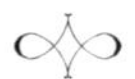

After hours at the station, my parents and I follow the Greenwoods back to her house. Lacy clings to me once inside the house as if she's afraid I'll leave her. I'm not going anywhere.

Things get especially awkward when her mom tries to take her upstairs to shower and change but she demands I go instead.

My gaze flits over to Mom's and she gives me a nod. Dad's jaw clenches but he doesn't argue otherwise. It's Stephanie I'll have to contend with.

"Steph—" I start.

"Just go. Please help her. I'll put on some coffee," she mutters.

I guide Lacy upstairs into the bathroom and hug her to me once the door closes. "Lace, I am so sorry."

She hugs me tighter. "I was so scared."

I kiss the top of her head. My body trembles with fury but I attempt to remain calm for her. "What did they do?"

"They were giving me a hard time. I managed to walk away from them but then they caught up. Bryce held me down against the wall while he said terrible things to me. Bobby kissed me and groped me. And then…" I tense as she lets out a ragged breath. "He forced his finger inside of me."

"I'm going to kill them, Lacy."

She tilts her head up and her eyes swim with tears. "Don't you dare. If you hurt them, you'll go to prison again. I need you here with me."

I kiss her mouth until we're both breathless. Then, I rest my forehead against hers. "I don't know what to do."

"Just stick with me. Our parents have our backs and we don't have to keep this private much longer. But just promise me you won't do anything to jeopardize our time together," she begs.

I nod my vow. "But I'm firing him. I don't care what his parents or the church say."

"Do you still even have a job to be able to fire him?" she murmurs.

I run my fingers through her silky hair and tug her head back so I can look at her teary blue eyes. "I hope so." I close my eyes for a moment. "I'm so sorry, Lace. I acted stupidly. I'd assumed we were alone.

The doors were locked…" I sigh. "I didn't think Bobby and his family would show up."

"Don't apologize," she tells me, irritation in her voice. "It happened and we were both on board. Everything was fine until those monsters…"

"Come on," I say gruffly and pull from her grasp to start the shower. I untie her dress and send it dropping to the floor. Once she's naked, I really notice the bruises starting to form on her forearms and on one of her breasts. It makes me want to hurt those bastards who put their hands on her.

I strip out of my clothes and join her under the hot spray. Gently, I wash away everywhere they touched her. I'm about to turn off the water when she reaches between us and grips my cock that is hard despite my not wanting it to be. I simply want to take care of her.

"I need this. I keep freaking out every time I think about him touching me there," she whispers as she starts stroking my dick. "Please."

"Are you hurt?"

"It burned when he did it because I was dry but my body can handle you making love to me, Easton. I *need* you to make love to me."

I grab her tiny ass and lift her up. Our mouths

connect and I kiss her with all the love I can possibly convey. Her slender legs wrap around my hips as I push her up against the wall. I'm gentle as I push into her tight heat. Her breath catches the moment I'm seated completely inside her.

"That's better," she whimpers. "So much better."

I nip at her lips in a greedy way. It makes me mental that those Johnston boys touched what's mine. And she is mine. I'm going to marry this girl one day, I just know it.

"Marry me, vixen," I blurt out against her mouth.

She laughs—the first one since this entire ordeal—and it warms me to my soul. "Was that a statement or a question?"

"You're going to marry me as soon as you can and you're going to let me love you until we're old," I tell her with a crooked grin.

Her blue eyes twinkle with happiness. "Well, since I don't have a say in it, I guess it's a done deal, huh?"

I thrust my hips into her making her moan probably louder than she should since our parents are downstairs. "Damn straight."

Our laughter and teasing die down as I pound

into her, as if I can thrust my promise all the way inside her to her heart. She comes with a sudden gasp and her pussy clenches around me like always. God, she's so perfect.

I groan and let out my release.

This time I don't bother pulling out because she's mine and I'm going to make her mine in every possible way.

TEN

Lacy

THE PAST THREE WEEKS HAVE BEEN TORTURE. Gossip in our small-town spreads like wildfire. Everywhere I go, the older people in this community stare at me with pity. As if Pastor McAvoy was the big bad wolf who raped me. I know it's the Johnstons who are spreading those rumors. After that fateful night, the Johnstons realized they didn't have a leg to stand on, and were unable to get Easton fired. His dad, Gregory, ran interference and said they were silly claims by a mentally unstable boy with an obsessive crush on me. And Bobby didn't help matters by showing up at the church asking where

"Lashey" was. I'd taken one look at him and started bawling my eyes out. All those memories came flooding back. It was apparent to anyone around me who the real criminal was around there. Gregory and another deacon escorted him from the property and he's been banned from coming back. His family, and several of their loyal friends, no longer come to church.

While I wait for Easton to meet me for lunch, I stare at the key fob in my hand. I still can't believe I'm driving now. After I lost the baby and Sean went to prison, I would have panic attacks in the car. Mom thought it unsafe to drive and my car has been garaged this entire time. But it was her, not long after the horrifying experience with the Johnstons, who gave me my car key back and suggested I start driving again. She hated the fact that I was alone waiting for her that night. I'd expected the anxieties to overwhelm me like they did before, but they didn't. Having a vehicle again was freeing. Plus, when it rains, Easton and I don't have to be cooped up in his house any longer.

My phone buzzes and I'm shocked to see it's from my ex-best friend, Olivia. Our friendship suffered when I went a little crazy with Sean and then with Nolan. And although we are cordial to each other, we haven't really hung out since. Seems like a lot of my friendships have fallen apart because of Sean and Nolan.

Olivia: Tonight a bunch of us are meeting up at club Orj-E for a party. It's a graduation party of sorts. Most of our class will be there including Ava. You should come.

I smile at the mention of my friend Ava. During my rough time when I was involved with Nolan, she came to my aide. She even got hurt trying to protect me from him. I feel indebted to her.

Me: Can I bring a date?

Olivia: Is he nice?

Me: He's a preacher, so yeah.

Olivia: OMG!!! You're dating a preacher?! You hussy! No wonder you started going to church!

I laugh at her response. This is what I miss.

Me: It was definitely motivating. I can't wait for you to meet him.

Olivia: Does he know you're inviting him to a sex club?

Me: My preacher is sometimes bad…

Olivia: OMG. Nine tonight. Use the back entrance since you're still underage. I can't wait to

see your dirty preacher. Is he old? Does he wear suspenders? Does he carry a Bible in his back pocket?

Me: Okay. Kinda. Nope. And nah, I look at his ass a lot…there's no Bible shielding that view.

Olivia: Hussy!

Me: I missed you.

My laughter falls away as my somber mood sets in. The three dots move and then stop. Move and then stop. Move and then a text.

Olivia: I missed you too. I'm glad I have my friend back.

The car door opens and I scream, dropping my phone between the console and the seat. Easton drops into the passenger seat, grinning wickedly at me.

"Hey, honey." He reaches forward and slides his palm around the back of my neck. When he pulls me to him, I go willingly. Always willingly. Our mouths connect for a kiss and his thumb strokes my neck in an affectionate way. "You ready to eat?"

"Always. I'm craving Moon Wok."

He laughs. "You're always craving Moon Wok. We've had it three times this week."

"Shhh," I say with a grin. "The cheese wontons

are calling my name. Lacy…Lacy…eat me…”

“All I heard was eat me,” he says with a growl as he palms my thigh and runs it up my skirt, his fingertips brushing against my panties underneath. “And *you're* something I'm always craving.” His breath his hot against mine. “I'm going to defile you right here in the parking lot, vixen. You're going to love it too.”

I lean my head back against the seat and thank God my windows are tinted. The naughty preacher works his fingers past my panties and into my body.

He's right. I love all the things he does to me.

I love when he's my good preacher.

But I also love it when he's my dirty criminal.

Who says you can't have the best of both worlds?

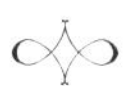

“Wow,” Easton mutters as he hugs me possessively to his side. “Just wow.”

I giggle and hug his middle. “We don't have to stay long. I know it's not your scene. I just miss Olivia.”

He kisses my temple. “Anywhere with you is my scene. We'll stay as long as you want. Just know I'm not sharing what's mine.”

We both stare in awe as three men grope at

a naked woman on a sofa. I've never been in club Orj-E before. It's a sex club that caters to people seeking their different kinks. The bouncer who let us in the back—and didn't ask for IDs which I'm thinking was on purpose—gave us a quick rundown on what to expect. Naked people everywhere doing naughty things. I got that message loud and clear.

"Lacy!" Olivia yells over the sensual music that's thumping through the club. "Isn't this place wicked?"

Behind her stands a brute, mountain of a man. Tall, solid, a dark beard. His possessiveness over Olivia is loud and clear. When she notices me staring, she laughs and points at him. "Miles owns this club. Miles, my friend Lacy and her preacher boyfriend."

"Easton," my preacher boyfriend says, offering his hand to the big guy.

"Glad to have you both here," Miles grunts back as he shakes Easton's hand. "Enjoy yourselves. You can always ask for forgiveness in the morning." He gives us a mischievous wink before walking over to the bar.

Olivia rolls her eyes but laughs. "You look good, Lace. You're glowing. Happiness always did look best on you. How's Steph?"

"She misses you," I tell her. "You should stop by

and have dinner with us one day. You're practically a daughter to her."

Guilt shines in Olivia's green eyes and she nods. "I promise, I will. Steph was always the mom I didn't have growing up. Too bad we were never successful on hooking her and Dad up."

I laugh and turn to Easton. "When we were fourteen, we wanted to be sisters and had this grand idea to play matchmaker. We snuck out to create this romantic picnic in Olivia's backyard once when I spent the night. The plan was to call my mom over there to come get me on the ruse I had a stomach ache. We got all the candles lit in the gazebo and I called Mom. Everything was going smoothly until the wind knocked over a candle onto the blanket where all the food was laid out. It went up in flames so fast."

Olivia chuckles. "Dad ran out freaking the hell out. You and I barely made it out of the gaze-bo unscathed! By the time your mom arrived, the entire thing was engulfed in flames. They spent the next three hours comparing punishments and who could yell the loudest. Steph and Dad didn't hook up romantically but they became good friends at that point and always made sure to call the other frequently when we were together to make sure we weren't up to anymore shenanigans."

"How is your dad anyway?" I ask.

Before she can answer, a man in only slacks and his sculpted bare chest on full display, shows up with a tray full of shots. My stomach churns when he offers me one. Easton takes two, one for each of us, but when I shake my head, he downs them both.

"I'm going to steal her away for a minute," Miles says once he's returned. "Nice meeting you two. We'll catch back up shortly. Check out the black room." He smirks and points at a door toward the back. "If you dare."

Curiosity niggles at me. When I glance up at Easton, I can tell he's wondering about it too. I'm about to ask him if he wants to go when he starts guiding me through the throng of dancing bodies to the room Miles pointed at.

We make it to the room and a bouncer lets us inside. It's pitch black when he closes the door. The music is different in here. Techno or something. It feels electric and as though it's pulsating through me to my bones. Someone touches my arm and I squeak. Easton pulls me to his side, his mouth to my ear.

"I think this is some sort of orgy room or something. Stay close," he growls.

We blindly make our way through people that seem to be everywhere when suddenly white light flashes like a lightning bolt. It illuminates the room for a brief moment before darkness blinds us again. Bodies. Tons of naked, dancing, writhing bodies. It makes me nervous until Easton pushes me up against a wall. With my back to it, I feel safer.

"I'm going to fuck you right here in front of all these people." His hot breath against the shell of my ear sends currents of heat surging to my core.

White light flashes again. I'm able to see his wild eyes for a moment before darkness shrouds us again. His palms slide up under my dress and he hooks his thumbs into my panties before dragging them down my thighs. I step out of them and immediately feel vulnerable and exposed. But his palms are all over my breasts, distracting me. His mouth finds my throat. Bite. Suck. Kiss. Nibble. He drives me insane with his teasing ways. My arousal is thick and making the inside of my thighs sticky with need.

"Fuck me, Preach. Do it now. I can hardly stand it."

He grabs my ass roughly and lifts me up so that

I'm shrieking in surprise. It takes him a minute to fumble with his jeans.

Flash.

I get a glimpse of his eyes. Feral. Untamed. Starved. And then he's pushing inside of me in one hard thrust. I cry out and latch onto his neck with my fingers. He bucks against me with all these strangers around us. I close my eyes and get lost in the moment. One hand remains at my ass to keep me upright but his other one roams over my breasts and to my throat. His clutch on me is firm and possessive. Tiny thrills shoot through me. I want him to squeeze me there. As if attuned to my needs, he does. His grip tightens enough to make me see stars in the dark space. My pussy clenches in response which in turn makes him thrust harder. Squeeze harder. Grab my ass harder.

Flash.

Behind my closed lids, I get a glimpse of white light until it's gone again. My orgasm is on the cusp of making me insane. So close. So close. He grips my throat even tighter and brushes his lips against mine. I can smell the spicy scent of liquor on his breath from the two shots he consumed. It makes me want to lick every corner of his mouth to taste it.

Flash.

And then I'm coming.

No screams because he has them literally caught in my throat.

All I can do is shudder, at his mercy, with pleasure until his own heat surges into me with an explosive intensity. His cum fills me up and selfishly I hope for a baby. We've been having unprotected sex for weeks now. It's only a matter of time.

"God, I love you," he growls, his forehead resting against mine.

"I love you too," I rasp out the moment he releases my throat.

He sets me to my feet but doesn't return my panties. Hot cum trickles down the inside of my thighs. I love the slippery feel when I rub my thighs together. His head is down as he tucks his cock away when hot breath is on my ear.

"Just can't stay away from the older men, can you, Lacy?"

My heated blood chills and freezes in my veins. Sean Polk.

"What will everyone think when I show them the video of you fucking the preacher? Will he go to prison too?" he sneers, his spittle spraying my ear.

His hand finds my breast through my dress and he gropes me painfully.

I open my mouth to scream.

Flash.

I see so much in one moment on Easton's handsome face.

Surprise. Confusion. Fury. Hate.

The darkness once again steals away my vision. But over the music, I can hear sickening crunches.

Pop. Crunch. Crack.

Flash.

Easton is on the ground, straddling Sean, and his powerful back is tense as his muscles flex before he delivers a punch.

Pop. Crunch. Crack.

Flash.

Blood on his fists. He pummels relentlessly.

I manage to get ahold of my senses and grab the back of his shirt. "Easton! No!"

He fights against me as he struggles to hit Sean again, but I manage to pull him back using all my weight. His massive body lands on top of mine. Rage ripples through him. I can feel it. Almost taste it.

Instead of letting him go, I hug him from behind. As much as I hate Sean, I refuse to let Easton go to prison for assaulting him.

Flash.

Sean staggers as he stands, blood coating his face. I notice his phone near his shoe—lit up with a video playing of Easton and I fucking—before darkness surrounds us again. Easton shoots up to his feet while I scramble over to where the video playing is the only light in the room. A bigger, stronger person beats me too it, nearly knocking me out of the way, and I screech in surprise.

Crunch. Crunch. Crunch.

Flash.

Easton stomps on Sean's phone over and over again.

Then, I'm getting hauled into the two protective arms I love so much.

"Let's get out of here, vixen."

ELEVEN

EASTON

"WHAT IF THEY DON'T APPROVE?" LACY asks, nerves making her voice quake.

I give her hand a squeeze as we make our way into my parents' house. "Of course they approve. I think they like you better than me."

She giggles but I meant what I said. Ever since that night when the Johnston boys assaulted her and my parents got involved, they've latched onto Lacy. I don't know any other way to explain it. Mom watches her like a guard dog at church and enjoys taking her and her mother out to lunch often. Dad spends a lot of time in prayer with her after church. I don't know what he says to her or what they pray about but she looks so serene. Both my parents adore her. The night after Lace and I showered at her house, my parents made it known that they didn't approve of our age difference and the illegal nature of our relationship. Not that age matters anymore now that she's legally old enough to make her own decisions. They did, however, approve of our love. And with Lacy, we have so much love, it's infectious.

"Oh, sweetheart," Mom says as she steps into the foyer. "You look gorgeous in that dress. Yellow brings out the blue in your eyes."

Lacy beams at her and then steps away from me to hug my mom. "Thank you, Lydia."

"Easton tells me we're celebrating something. Did my boy treat you right this past weekend in the city?" Mom questions.

I smirk and Lacy sends me a warning glare. I treated her real nice when I pinned her against the bathroom sink at the hotel I booked for us—while we were in New York City—with her blonde hair in my brutal grip and forced her to watch me as I fucked her from behind. It was erotic as hell.

"He always treats me better than I deserve,"

Lacy breathes.

I laugh and give my mom a hug. "She deserves much more than me but I'm thankful she's a blonde and hasn't come to that conclusion yet."

She elbows me and Mom gives me a pinch. "You're insufferable, son."

"I'm teasing," I say with a wicked grin. "Lace is the smartest girl I know. Did you tell Mom what you did?"

They know we went to New York for the weekend, but they think it was a romantic getaway. And while it *was* romantic, that wasn't the real reason we'd gone.

Lacy's cheeks burn bright—and it's not for the fact that she's not wearing panties under her dress. "I finished *Mikey the Majestic*."

Mom's eyes brighten. "Oh, how wonderful. When do I get to read the rest?" It warms my heart that Lacy shared her story with both our moms.

"Actually," Lacy murmurs, her throat burning bright red. "It's with an editor."

"At a publishing house," I finish for my modest girl. "We met with the publisher on Saturday. They picked up *Mikey the Majestic* and better yet they want her to turn it into a series. A five-book deal, Mom. Lace didn't want to say anything until we knew for sure."

Lacy had been worried when I suggested she submit it to a publisher. We scoped out some that fit her story, researched them to make sure they were legit, and then she wrote a letter explaining the emotions and heartache that went into writing her book. A reputable publisher snagged her up in a hurry. She was shocked. I sure as hell wasn't.

"Oh my word," Mom gasps in delight. "This is wonderful news. A time for celebration!"

She hurries from the room calling for Dad. Lacy turns and smiles at me. Despite all the crap she's been through, Lacy is strong and resilient. She survived Sean Polk, Nolan Jenkins, and the Johnston boys. All men who saw her innocence as a weakness. Something to be devoured and destroyed.

"You heard, Mom. Time to celebrate," I tell her as I snag her wrist and pull her to me. I kiss her forehead as she brings her hand between us.

"We didn't even get to this part yet," she murmurs.

The diamond engagement ring on her finger glimmers beneath the foyer chandelier. I'd given it to her last night before I nearly plowed her into the hotel mirror. That's how *we* celebrate.

I tuck her into my side and then walk her into the kitchen where Mom is babbling to Dad about Lacy's book deal. He's listening intently, pride shining in his eyes.

As my parents gush over my future wife, I can't help but smile. Several weeks ago, we closed the Sean chapter of her life. We went straight to Sheriff McMahon and told him about Sean violating his restraining order. He located him that night and arrested him. The trial went quick once testimonies came out that Lacy wasn't the only one he stalked after his release. He terrorized his ex-girlfriend who had his baby, as well as a few other girls he'd touched against their will when he was their guidance counselor. Judge Maximillian Rowe seemed almost gleeful to announce that Sean Polk was going back to prison.

And I certainly was not.

It still worries me that I blacked out that night. When Lacy and I got into the car afterwards, I'd come out of my haze. She had to explain all that happened. I went black with rage, much like I'd done against those three men in prison, and beat his face to a bloody pulp. Lacy says she likes knowing I can go into Hulk Mode—her words, not mine—when she's threatened.

"The Johnstons put up a 'for sale' sign in the yard last week," Mom tells me, jerking me from my inner thoughts.

My eyebrows raise to my hairline. "That so?"

Dad nods. "Bobby apparently confessed what happened to them. It wasn't until they received Lacy's letter though that they put the house on the market."

I glance over to her and peace shines on her face. "What did you say?" I ask.

She bites on her plump bottom lip for a moment. "I told Jennifer in detail what happened. How terrified I was. But…" She looks over at my dad and he nods. "I told her I forgave them. Bryce and Bobby for hurting me. Jennifer and Jay for taking their sons' side versus the woman they victimized. I feel better getting that off my chest."

My sweet, brave, beautiful girl.

"I'm proud of you," I tell her, my lips quirking on one side. She reaches for me and my mom gasps. We get intercepted as my mom snags her hand.

"Easton! You proposed to her?" Mom shrieks.

Lacy and I both laugh. "I sure did," I tell her, a

smug grin on my lips. "She even said yes, believe it or not."

Dad chuckles and grips my shoulder. "You're quite the catch," he says, pride in his voice. "At least that's what she tells me every chance she gets."

The rest of dinner is full of laughter, family, and fun. Even her mom shows up in time for dessert. Steph fusses over Lacy and with good reason. I can't stop fussing over her either. Eventually my mom, ever the perceptive one, lifts a brow in question.

"We're not done celebrating yet are we?" she asks.

Steph beams happily and shakes her head. "Not even close."

I sit down on the couch in the living room and tug Lacy into my lap. Steph sits beside us while my parents find their recliners. My palms protectively rub over Lacy's still small stomach.

"You guys are going to be grandparents."

"They handled that well," Lacy says as she exits my bathroom, a towel wrapped around her supple body.

My eyes are glued to the way her tits are barely contained in the towel. They've already started growing in the few weeks she's been pregnant. I can't wait to watch her body change and grow as it accommodates our baby.

"You're giving me the look." Her hands are on her hips and she arches a golden eyebrow up at me. Blonde hair that is usually golden and lighter, is darker being that it's wet. She doesn't look so innocent with that pouty bottom lip trapped between her teeth.

"What look?" I feign innocence. We all know I'm guilty.

"That look. The *I'm going to devour you very shortly* look."

Smirking, I shrug and sit up to peel off my T-shirt. "I *am* going to devour you very shortly."

"You're insatiable, Preach."

"Stop being so delicious, honey."

She beams at me. "I love you but are you sure you want me here?"

My brows furl together. "Of course I want you here. You're going to be my wife and you're carrying my baby. The only place you belong is here with me. From here on out."

Her nervousness fades away as she walks over to the dresser that is now half filled with her things.

Steph had been sad when Lacy moved in with me not even two days after we ran into Sean at the club. I think she'd seen the seriousness of me wanting to care for and love her daughter until the end of our existence. I did, however, ask Steph's blessing when I wanted to propose to Lacy. She cried, took my cheeks in her palms, and told me thank you for bringing her daughter back to her.

Lacy pulls a pair of silky purple panties from the drawer and drops her towel. My dick thickens and strains against my boxers seeing her perfectly round ass. I don't know why she bothers with panties. I'm just going to take them off. I like seeing her bare and ready as often as possible. She gracefully slides them up her thighs. When she finishes, she turns to me. Tears shimmer in her eyes. My boner softens as worry niggles at me.

"Come here," I growl.

She runs over to me and straddles my hips on the bed. I hug her to me so that our bare chests are pressed together.

"What's wrong?"

"I'm so happy. You make me happy."

I chuckle. "Happiness is a good thing, Lace." Her list of things that make her happy is so long now that she has devoted a notebook to adding in entries. It's something I sneak a look at often. At least once a day. Seeing what makes *her* happy makes *me* happy.

"What if God takes this baby too?"

I squeeze her and kiss her temple. "God doesn't take babies," I murmur. "You know this."

She nods. "I'm just scared."

"Have a little faith, honey. Everything is going to work out. I promise."

"How can you be so sure?"

"With a love like this, how could it not?"

She lifts up and stares at me with such adoration it'd knock me over if I weren't already lying down. Her body rises as she sits on her knees. An offering. I'll take it because I'm starved for anything she gives me. With a growl in my throat, I hook my finger into her panties and pull them to the side revealing her smooth pussy. She works my aching cock out of my boxers and positions it at her entrance. Then, she slides down until she's completely seated on my cock.

Pleasure zings through my body but it's the look of unfiltered love on her pretty face that has my heart feeling as though it's just been zapped.

She fills up parts of me that were empty.

She makes me sin when I've vowed not to.

She loves me so hard and I'll die trying to prove that I love her even more.

As she starts rocking on me, my entire body seems to flood with a peaceful sensation. She and I, we were meant to be. Always a part of the big, complicated plan. The big man upstairs knew what he was doing.

Love finds a way.

Love always wins.

Love is everything.

I clutch her beautiful neck and pull her to me. Our mouths crash, her teeth nicking my lip, and we kiss as though it will be our last.

But it won't be our last.

It'll be the first of many.

This was always his plan. A broken girl and an ex-convict. Two people who were just jagged enough that they slotted together perfectly in a way no other two people could.

God works in mysterious ways.

EPILOGUE

Lacy

One year later…

"Can you grab Elias's binky?" I ask Easton.

He reaches into the diaper bag and retrieves the pacifier. Elias, now drunk on breastmilk, can barely keep his eyes open. He happily accepts his binky before his eyes fall shut. Sometimes I stare at him for hours. Especially in the middle of the night while Easton sleeps. Elias—with the same blue-green eyes as his daddy—is a miracle in our life. I understand now that God doesn't take. He gives.

"You're crying." Easton's voice is gruff and it startles Elias. "What's wrong?"

I turn my eyes to my husband and blink away the silly tears. "Nothing. I'm just so thankful we have him."

He leans over and kisses my mouth. "Me too, honey. Me too."

Mom strolls into her living room carrying a basket of towels to fold. We came over to visit after church. She's always good for a Sunday home-cooked meal. Especially after she and I tag team in the church nursery. Caring for all those babies—including my own—is taxing but I wouldn't change a thing. Despite not seeing my husband preach to his steadily growing congregation, I enjoy being in the church nursery rotation.

Easton sets to texting with his friend Dane. My gaze drifts to my mom. Today she's beautiful, still in her church dress. She spends a lot of time at the gym keeping her figure. Where I've softened in areas due to childbirth, Mom remains tight and fit. She really is a knockout with her long golden-blonde hair, flawless makeup, and form fitting outfits that compliment her body. The spiked heels she wears make her at least four inches taller and elongate her already long slender legs.

My mom is gorgeous.

Ding-dong!

Elias startles and whimpers. Mom hurries to the door. My gaze follows after her as she swings open the door. Anthony Blakely stands on the other side of the door. When did that kid get so big? His hulking frame fills the doorway. Mom takes a step away from him. Anthony, despite his imposing body all muscles and hard lines, is harmless though.

"Anthony Blakely?" Mom questions, astonished. "I had you confused for Quinn there for a moment."

Anthony gives her a crooked grin. "Dad doesn't like that I'm taller than him."

She laughs—no, she giggles—as she steps aside. "Please, come in. Is there something you needed?"

He saunters into the foyer. When he sees me, he waves. "Hey, Lace."

"Hey, Anthony." We went to school together all our lives. Anthony is a couple of years behind me. At almost seventeen, he's every bit a man as his father or my husband.

"I was next door at Mrs. Sing's when I noticed your yard," he tells Mom, his hands on his hips.

Anthony is built like your typical high school

football player god. Massive. Muscly. Cocky. His almost black hair hangs down over one of his eyebrows giving him a playful look. Anyone who knows Anthony, though, knows he's anything but playful. His twin brother Aiden is the playful one. Anthony is broody and grumpy. Again, just like his father.

"What *about* my yard?" Mom questions in defense.

"Whoever you're paying to do it, you should fire." Anthony darts his gaze over to Easton in question.

Easton laughs and raises both palms. "Don't look at me. I offered and was told no."

"*I* do the yard," Mom huffs. Her shoulders are stiff as she's no longer happy to see him. Irritation has her lips pursing together. "Nothing is wrong with it."

Anthony snorts. "You cut the grass way too short for one. The edging isn't straight. And do you know the difference between a weed and a flower? Your garden doesn't."

Mom gapes at him and I can't help but giggle.

"Oh, boy," I mutter under my breath.

The stupid guy keeps on running his mouth. "It's the worst looking yard on the street. Pales in comparison next to Mrs. Sing's. Surely you've noticed how nice her yard looks?"

Mom's cheeks blaze bright red and I wonder why. I've noticed Anthony mowing next door before in just a pair of basketball shorts. When you're married to the Adonis I am though, nothing compares. But the guilty flash in my mom's eyes tells me she notices him. A lot.

"It's okay," Mom lies. She's told me on more than one occasion that Mrs. Sing has a nice yard.

Anthony laughs. "It's better than okay. It's the best."

Mom swipes at a rogue blonde strand of hair from her eyes—clearly flustered—and lets out a sigh of annoyance. "So you came over here to tell me what a crap job I do on my yard? Thanks."

His grin is wolfish. "I came to see if you'd hire me."

At this, Mom scoffs. "You're just like your dad. Arrogant and presumptuous. Of course I won't hire you. Not only do you have the worst business spiel known to man, but I also can't afford you."

More lies.

Mom does well at her advertising firm.

Anthony shrugs. "I'll do it for free." His brows

furrow. "Well, not exactly free. A trade. I need something from you in return."

Mom's face turns even brighter crimson. She shoots me a confused look. Easton chuckles from beside me.

"What do you want from me?" Mom's voice has risen a few octaves.

Anthony pauses for a long time. His gaze unabashedly peruses along her curves before he meets her stare with a conspiratorial grin. "One thing."

"W-What?"

He smirks. "I need you to get me an internship at your agency. Dad won't let me intern at his company because he wants me to bring some different experiences to the table. Plus, the college I'm eyeing likes when you volunteer. Dad thinks it would be a conflict of interest if my only experience interning was with him." His brows tug together in a puppy dog stare. I bite back a laugh because he clearly doesn't know my mom. She's seconds away from throttling him for being a little shit.

"Okay."

My smile falls away. I'm stunned. "What?" I ask, my voice coming out a choke of surprise.

Mom lifts her chin. "We need an intern. Quinn

Blakely's son would be a good fit if Anthony here has one iota of his father's work ethic and drive." She sighs and flutters her fingers at him. "And I do need a yard boy."

Anthony growls. "I'm not a boy."

Easton and I share a knowing look. No, Anthony is certainly not a boy. He looks like he's perfectly capable of throwing my mom over his shoulder and carrying her upstairs. The thought has trickles of excitement surging through me.

"She needs a pool guy too," I pipe up. "Javier forgets to come half the time and does a crappy job."

"Lacy!" Mom admonishes. "I don't need—"

"I'll do anything you want," Anthony murmurs, his voice low and promising.

It shuts Mom up. She shoots me a helpless stare and I shrug.

"Looks like you have a job, Anthony," I say with a grin.

"From the sounds of it," Easton chimes in. "Like three *free* jobs. Good luck with that. If you're in the business of working for free, the church could always use an extra pair of hands to polish those pews. They sure do get dirty."

I shoot him a warning glare. We have only had

sex in the sanctuary the one time, but it's a time we'll never forget. That moment was the catalyst for… everything.

"I'll think about it," Anthony tells Easton before turning his attention to Mom. He juts out his massive arm and offers his hand. "Do we have a deal?"

Mom's tiny hand gets swallowed in his. He's a mountain compared to her. I've always thought of her as feisty and larger than life. Right now, she's a fair maiden about to be devoured by the giant in her tale.

"You can let go now," Mom rasps as she tries to tug away her hand.

Anthony's features darken. "It's a three-part deal. The handshake takes at least three times longer to seal the deal."

He doesn't let her go.

And a part of me hopes he never does.

Anthony Blakely is nothing but trouble.

Mom needs a little trouble now that her little girl is no longer finding it around every corner.

"Do you see what I see?" Easton questions, his hot breath close to my ear. Elias sighs in his sleep and I absently stroke his dark hair.

"I see, Preach."

"Do I need to kick his ass?"

At this, I laugh. "Nah, she's got it covered." My mom jerks her hand away and points at the door.

"Time to go, Anthony. You can come over tomorrow. Be prepared to sweat." She tries her best to look threatening but fails miserably.

"I look forward to you making me sweat, Ms. Greenwood," he murmurs as he heads toward the door. He casts a heated glance at her over his shoulder. "All. Day. Long."

He leaves and it isn't until the door slams shut that Mom let's out an exasperated cry.

"This was a bad idea, huh?" Her panicked eyes meet mine.

Easton shrugs. "Everyone deserves a chance to prove themselves."

She kicks off her heels and storms off to her bedroom, clearly still in a panic about hiring a good-looking football player teenager. It's a recipe for disaster. Good thing Mom knows her way around a kitchen.

"They're going to fuck," Easton murmurs, his eyes gleaming wickedly.

"Preachers can't say fuck," I scoff.

He smirks. "Church nursery workers can't say

fuck either," he challenges.

I smile and shake my head. "We have much to be forgiven for, Preach."

"I'm going to take you home and we'll add a few more naughty things to the list. Go big or go home, honey."

Leaning forward, I kiss his full lips. "Lead the way, sinner. The night is still young."

Lots of growling and stuffing items into a diaper bag before we're loaded up and headed home. My preacher man is a man of his word. And he's about to make good on his promise. All. Night. Long.

As we drive, I bask in the happiness that seems to follow me like a thousand rays of sunshine after a rainy day. My series with the publisher about Mikey is doing well. My husband is hot and adoring and perfect in every way. Our son is adorable and a good baby.

Life is better than I could have ever imagined.

And I can't wait to see what God has in store for us next.

The End

Bonus Story

TIME SERVED

A Taboo Treat

by K Webster

PART ONE

Deputy Gentry Adair

"Gentry Adair," Jessie hisses from inside the jail cell, tossing her long blonde hair over her shoulder like the typical high school cheerleader she is. "I'm going to kill you."

I snort and shake my head at her. "You can't threaten a cop. It's illegal."

Her perfect lip curls up, baring her teeth, as she glares at me. "Illegal? This"—she motions around her—"is illegal. Besides, you're not even a real cop. You're just my brother's lame-ass best friend." She crosses her arms over her ample chest, which is barely contained in her sunny yellow dress with a plunging halter-top neckline. Her nostrils flare with fury. Sweet little Jessie Bennett grew up into one helluva sexy spitfire, didn't she?

"This," I say with a tap of my finger to the badge on my belt, "says I'm real. These"—I jangle the handcuffs—"say I'm real." I laugh and flash her a grin. "You were a bad girl, and I did my job." I'm the only one here at this hour in our small-town precinct. Nobody to interfere with my devious plans.

"Goddammit, I hate you."

I quirk a brow at her. "Really? Because two years ago, when you could have gotten my ass sent to prison, you begged me to fuck you. That offer still stand?"

If looks could kill, I'd be dead right now. Her icy blue eyes are hard and furious. "I want my phone call, asshole." Those plump lips of hers are bitable as hell. I remember when they used to smile for me—bright and adoring. Once upon a time, she was an annoying kid who had a crush on me. Then, one day, she was a pretty young woman who would give me blue balls just by walking in the room with her coy smiles and flirtatious grins. But completely off limits. Now, though, she's finally fucking legal. About damn time.

I saunter over to the landline on my desk and unplug it from the wall. "Oops. It's broken." When I turn back around, her anger has faded some and confusion has set in.

"What are you doing?" she huffs and throws her hands on her curvy hips. "Are you just fucking with me or what?"

I stalk back over to her and lick my lips. Soon, I'll have her taste smeared all over my tongue. Mark my words. This has been a long time coming.

"Oh, sweetness, I do have plans for you…" I trail off and regard her with a smoldering grin. Her anger completely fades as she lets her gaze roam down the front of my body. When her eyes land on my cock—which is extremely happy to see her and stiff in my slacks—she lets out a gasp of surprise. Those icy blues of hers are heated when they dart back up to mine. I love how her neck turns bright red, just like it used to whenever I'd come over to her house to see my best friend Joey. The girl followed me around like a lost puppy.

I behaved myself then because I was seven years her senior.

Also, because my best friend would have murdered me for touching his sister.

But Joey's working in Chicago now, and Jessie's finally eighteen.

No more waiting. No more rules. No more obstacles standing in my way.

When I start tugging at the knot of my tie, her eyes widen.

"What are you doing?"

"I'm taking off my tie. What are you doing?" I challenge with a smirk.

"I'm being unlawfully held by a douchebag on my birthday," she sasses, her bottom lip jutting out in the cutest fucking pout. I'm going to bite that lip.

I toss the tie away and start unbuttoning my uniform shirt. She begins fanning her face. This girl, who's wanted this for as long as I can remember, suddenly doesn't look so sure of herself. I'll just have to convince her.

"You should spend your birthday with me, anyway. Those friends of yours don't know you like I do," I tell her, my voice dropping to a low growl. Earlier, when my buddy James called to tell me the bar was crammed full of underage girls, drinking for Jessie's eighteenth birthday, I was furious and knew what I had to do. I didn't care about the other girls. Just one. Mine.

"You don't know me at all," she tries, her voice shaking.

I lift a brow at her as I peel off my shirt and toss it to the floor. "Oh," I say as though I'm confused. "I thought you wanted me." She and I both know that's the fucking truth.

"You thought wrong," she lies, her nostrils flaring as her eyes greedily skim over my sculpted chest, which is barely covered by my wife beater.

I stalk over to the cell and gesture her closer. "Come say that to my face, liar."

The dress she's wearing leaves little to the imagination. It's tight and practically fucking see-through. I'm so glad I stole her away from all the leering eyes at the bar. I can see her perfect nipples perking up through the fabric—nipples I'm going to bite and suck until they're tender and sore.

"I don't want you," she hisses as she stomps forward. Her hands grab the bars as she leans in so she can glower at me. "I. Don't. Want. You."

With lightning speed, I reach forward and snag her neck in my grip. Her gorgeous blue eyes widen in shock when I pull her face against the wide-set bars. She's so tiny, I bet if she tried, she could wriggle herself through them. Pink, supple lips are parted between the bars—just waiting to be sucked and worshipped.

"Lie to me again, sweetheart," I growl.

She whimpers when I stroke the side of her neck with my thumb. "I…"

Leaning into her, I brush my nose against hers. "What's that, Jessie?"

"I…"

"You want me to kiss you?" I quip, my lips grazing softly against hers. My cheekbones protest against the metal bars but it doesn't stop me from getting to my prize. Just enough room to reach what's mine.

She mewls and lets out the sexiest sound of approval. I don't wait for actual words and lean forward to kiss the mouth I've been dying to devour for two long years. Lips that belonged to me, but I wasn't allowed to touch. And, goddamn, are they sweet as hell. My palm slides down the front of her chest, and I cup her full tit, letting my thumb drag across her peaked nipple. A moan of pleasure escapes her, so I take the moment to deepen the kiss. Her tongue isn't shy and meets mine with a greedy eagerness that matches my own. Our kiss is heated and not fucking enough. I need so much more from her…

I slide my hand down her taut stomach toward the place that's been as forbidden as the apple in the damn garden of Eden. I'm going to devour that fruit. And I'm going to fucking enjoy every second of it.

My hand slips up under her dress, and I'm pissed to find her naked underneath. I let out a growl as I slide my finger between her wet pussy lips, locating her throbbing clit. A whimper escapes her, but I consume it along with her plump bottom lip. As I tease her pussy, I pull away from her, but not before nipping at her lip first. When I regard her, her mouth is red and swollen. Her eyes swimming with lust. Fuck, she's hot.

"Why did you wear this shit? Who were you trying to fuck?" I demand and not so gently pinch her clit.

She shudders with desire but flashes me a fiery glare. "You never wanted it," she bites out but then moans again when I slide a finger inside her tight channel. "I-I figured s-someone else would—oh God!"

I fuck her dripping pussy with my finger while grinding the heel of my hand against her clit. It drives her wild because she quivers so much I wonder if she'll collapse. But her white-knuckled grip on the bars tells me she's along for the ride until the end.

Hang on, sweetness, this ride goes all night.

She comes with a shriek that has my cock straining painfully against my uniform slacks. The moment she comes down from her high, I slip my hand out of her and bring my wet finger to my lips. I smear her juices across my mouth and then dart my tongue out to taste her.

So. Fucking. Sweet.

I glare and point at her with my wet finger. "Let's get something straight right now. I wanted you when I wasn't supposed to. And now that I'm allowed to have you, I'm going to have every god-damned part of you. Get ready, sweetness, I'm just getting started."

PART TWO

Little Jessie Bennett

Oh. My. God.

Gentry Adair just kissed and then fingerfucked me!

I shouldn't be so excited, considering he did this after he locked me up in a stupid cell, but I can't help it. A dream I've been fantasizing over for as long as I can remember has finally come true. *Happy birthday to me.*

The man has always been sexy, but it wasn't until he graduated from the police academy and became our town's deputy that he became unbelievably hot. It has to be the uniform. Yet…he's slowly removing items from his belt and losing said uniform quickly.

And the man is getting more good looking by the second. There goes that theory…

"We're going to fuck right there on that cot," he tells me with a smug crooked grin that would soak my panties, if I were wearing any. Gentry has always had this effect on me. So many times when he'd come over to hang out with my brother, I'd end up in my room later touching myself to thoughts of him making love to me.

"Are you this bossy with every woman you're with?" I demand, jealousy making my words come out with a bite.

He laughs and sheds his wife beater. Dear God, those abs are carved from stone. I lick my lips and shoot him a desperate look. One that says, *please fuck me and then let me spend hours nibbling on your pecs.*

"Actually," he murmurs as his brown eyes fall to my breasts that are bouncing with each heavy breath I take. "I only enjoy bossing you around."

"Gee, I feel so special," I smart off in a wry tone.

He unhooks his keys from his belt and stalks over to the cell door. His eyes are dark and hooded when he speaks. "You'll feel really special in about a minute when I have my tongue inside your sweet pussy."

I gape at him in shock, but I'll be damned if I don't shiver in anticipation. So many times, I heard Joey and him speak crudely about girls, but not once were Gentry's words aimed at me.

Until now.

And, dear baby Jesus, every ounce of heat the man possesses is obliterating me with each look. Each word. Each touch.

He unlocks the cell and saunters in, overpowering the space. Gentry and Joey played high school and college football. Gentry passed my brother on height and size long ago. This man towers over me with broad shoulders that look good enough to take a bite out of.

"Take off your dress, sweetheart," he instructs, his tongue darting out to lick his bottom lip. "I need to see my present."

At this, I smile. "It's *my* birthday, punk. I should be the one getting gifts here."

He grabs my wrist, the heat of his grip nearly scalding me, and drags my hand to where his cock is hard in his pants. "Happy birthday. I hope you like big gifts."

I let out a laugh that's half amused and half nervous. "I'm more of a jewelry girl. Just so you know for next time."

Both of his hands slide up to my neck where he reaches under my hair and unties my dress. Then, with sure movements, he pulls it down to reveal my full breasts. My dress slides to the floor, pooling at my ankles. The hungry way with which he admires my breasts has me gripping his cock through his pants. He lets out a pained groan. His dark eyes go wild with need—a look that I certainly want to see more of. My eyes meet his for a moment, and I lick my lips.

"I want to suck your cock," I whisper.

His glare becomes murderous, and I wonder if I said something wrong. But the words that come out next snuff out all apprehension. "Could you be any fucking hotter, sweetness? I'm dying to have your pretty lips wrapped around my dick."

I beam at him as I start unfastening his belt and slacks. They fall to the floor heavily, and I waste no time shoving his black boxer briefs down his thighs, so I can see his cock. I'm no prude and have seen many cocks on television and Tumblr.

Maybe I'm biased, but this is the best-looking

dick I've ever seen.

Long and thick enough that I know he's going to tear me apart. But smooth and silky enough that at least I know it'll be a soft destruction.

The concrete is cold on my knees, but when I look up at him, his fiery gaze is so intense, it could melt me to the floor. I grip his length, tentatively licking the salty tip. A hiss escapes him. My nerves calm down once I realize I'm the one in control now. The smug asshole has a death grip on my hair, and his entire body trembles when I take him deeper in my mouth. I rub the underside of his shaft with my tongue as I attempt to ease him into my throat. All my friends talk about is how good it feels for a man when you deep throat him. And I sure as hell want to give Gentry a blow job he'll never forget.

"Goddammit," he hisses. "I knew you'd be perfect."

His words spur me on, and I slide up and down his cock furiously until his heat is rushing down my throat without warning. He grips my hair as he fucks my face a couple of brutal times. Then, as if he gets ahold of his senses, he lets out a string of curse words.

"Fuck, sweetheart." He cradles my face in his

palms as I pull away from his wet cock. His brown eyes are soft and concerned. "Did I hurt you?"

I shake my head and give him a wicked smile. "Not yet." And it's the truth because my fantasy come to life is about to take my virginity. His cock is massive, so I know it's going to be painful.

He pulls me to my feet and hugs me to him. Our mouths meet for another heated kiss. With our naked bodies smashed together, I'm in a state of euphoria like I've never known before. I've only been in love with one boy. It'd always been unrequited. *Or so I thought.* A silent animal just waiting to be fed. I've been desperately hungry for him since the first time I saw him playing football in my front yard with no shirt on so many years ago. I'd been almost eleven when I developed my first crush—a crush that never went away. That seventeen-year-old boy just continued to grow more and more manly by the day. Other guys pursued me over the years, but I had no interest whatsoever.

My heart was set on Gentry Adair.

My heart still only beats for him.

When his palms find my ass, I let out a sigh of pleasure. My hands curl around the back of his neck so I can kiss him harder. The fire that always consumes me when it comes to this man is blazing out of control. I need him more than anything in my life.

"You're mine, sweetheart," he murmurs against my mouth. His words are like a song I've always wanted to hear. He lifts me and my legs wrap around his bare hips. When he stalks forward and presses my back against the cinderblock wall, I cry out from the cold.

"Shhh," he coos, his mouth attacking my neck and earlobe. "I'll warm you up." His cock is hot and throbbing as it bobs against the crack of my ass. Thrills shoot through me each time it touches me.

He holds my ass up with one hand and then reaches between us to grip his cock. Our eyes meet when he teases my wet opening with the tip.

"You ready for me?"

I bite my lip. A shiver ripples through me, and I can't tell if it's from the cold or nerves. "I think so. It's my first time."

His brown eyes become melted chocolate as he snares me in his heated gaze. "You saved yourself for me?"

I look away, embarrassment threatening to swallow me whole.

“Look at me,” he growls.

I snap my eyes back to meet his. Shame seems to have a grip around my throat as I choke out my words. “I-I was h-hoping it would be with you—”

“Good girl,” he praises, not letting me finish my words. “Don’t be afraid. I’m going to take care of you.”

His words soothe me and I nod. “Will it hurt?”

“Maybe,” he admits with a frown. “But I promise you I’m going to do my best to make it feel good.” His nose nuzzles against mine in an intimate way that seems to have a direct effect on my heart.

He breaks our gaze so he can focus on pushing his cock slowly into me. I’m wet and my body seems to crave him as much as I do because I slide halfway down his length without much resistance. He’s thick enough that it burns as he stretches me as wide as my body will go.

“I’ve loved you for far longer than I want to admit,” he whispers against my mouth. His words cause my heart to explode with happiness. Then, fire burns through me when he thrusts the rest of the way inside of me. A scream is lodged in my throat and two tears leak out of my eyes. I’m so stunned by the sudden onset of fiery pain that I stiffen in his grip. But then his fingers are massaging my still-swollen clit, making me quickly forget the fire between my legs. The burn quickly evolves into something that feels incredible. We're connected. And whole. Finally.

"Such a good girl," he murmurs, slowly rocking inside me. The pain is subsiding as pleasure fights for front and center.

He's not wearing a condom and somehow that makes this moment more special for me. Gentry isn't the type to put my health in danger. I trust that he wouldn't have sex with me bare unless he knew it was safe for him to do so. But I do have to tell him something he isn't going to like to hear.

"I'm not on birth control," I whimper, my voice overcome with emotion and desire.

My words seem to unleash the animal within him because he fucks me harder against the cinder-block wall and his mouth owns me with a soul-consuming kiss. I lose all sense of reality as I get swept up in our carnal lovemaking. The grip I have on his neck tightens when another orgasm begins to quake through me. White blissful stars glitter my line of vision, causing me to go blind with all the pleasure rippling through me.

His heat surges inside of me. I've never felt so connected to someone in all my life. I want to tether my heart to his, never letting go. He grunts as his cock seems to double in size. A few more thrusts and he slows. Our eyes meet. Darkness and love and possessiveness flicker in his gaze. I hope mine mirrors his.

"We probably shouldn't have done that," I murmur and bite on my bottom lip. "That was reckless."

"I told you that you were mine now." His forehead rests against mine. "I'm going to take care of you, just like I promised."

PART THREE

Deputy Gentry Adair

She's mine.

It's been that way since the year she turned sixteen—when she nearly pushed me over the edge of sanity. I remember it like it was yesterday. The way she climbed on top of me in the middle of the night when I'd stayed over at Joey's after I had a little too much to drink. Somehow, through the fog of my drunkenness, I'd found the power to tell her no. Hardest fucking thing I've ever done. I had this sexy little thing rubbing against me and begging for sex. Like the gentleman I was, I resisted.

I'm no gentleman now.

She lets out a surprised shriek when I grip her

ass and slide her off my cock that's already trying to get hard again. Jessie Bennett is like a miracle drug for my dick. I'm already eager to fuck her once more. But first, I need to take care of her.

"Time to clean you up, sweetheart," I tell her softly and smile at her as I lie her back on the cot.

Her blue eyes twinkle with love and happiness. She's much more relaxed than she was when I first hauled her in here, kicking and screaming.

"Spread your legs and let me see your sore pussy," I order with a flirtatious grin. "I want to make you feel better."

Her brows furrow together, but like the good girl she is, she parts her thighs for me. I kneel at the far end of the cot and admire her red, glistening sex. My cum drips from her raw-looking lips, soaking into the cot below. I bet my cum mixed with hers is fucking delicious.

"I'm going to kiss you," I growl as I lean forward and inhale her between her legs. Her scent is alluring as hell. Now that I've gotten a proper whiff of her, I'd be able to locate this perfect pussy anywhere. Like Toucan Sam, I'll follow my goddamned nose until my tongue is buried inside her.

Her breath hitches when my lips press a soft

kiss on her clit. I'm gentle as I love her pussy with just my mouth. Soft and tentative. My tongue is greedy, though, and refuses to be easy. The moment I run it along her seam and taste her orgasm mixed with mine, I become ravenous. I spear my tongue inside her tight hole, reveling in the cries of pleasure that rip from her.

"Gentry," she moans, her fingers gripped tightly in my hair. "Don't stop."

As if I will ever stop. Now that I've had her, there will never be any stopping. She's mine until the end. The slurping sounds would be vulgar to most ears, but to mine, they sound like music I need to hear more of. My grunts and her whimpers of pleasure are a symphony of longing getting slaughtered by love.

No more waiting.

No more wishing.

We can be together.

Her body is writhing on the cot so much that if I didn't have her pussy pinned down with my mouth, she'd probably roll right off it and onto the floor. Once I break my girl out of jail, I'm going to give her a proper lovemaking in my bed.

Until then, she'll get this desperate,

long-overdue fucking.

My teeth tug gently at her clit and it's enough to have her screaming. Somewhere amidst her strangled cry is an orgasm. Her body shakes violently. She'd admitted to being a virgin, and I hope to God she never made herself come this way. I want to be the only one to own that title. To be the one who makes her lose her mind with ecstasy. When she comes off her high, I lift up and admire my blonde beauty. Her eyes are closed and a smile plays at her lips. Most beautiful thing I've ever seen in this lifetime.

"You're coming home with me tonight," I tell her as my palm roams up her smooth stomach to her jiggling breast. "You're coming home with me every night."

Her features are soft as she regards me with a powerful look of love. It blazes in her eyes, so overwhelming I'm nearly burned by it. I take her hand and pull her into a sitting position. My lips press against the back of her hand.

"I have a present for you," I tell her. "Get dressed and I'll show you."

"I thought your cock was my present," she says with a laugh.

“My cock is most definitely the gift that keeps on giving,” I joke. “But I actually have a real present for you.”

Her eyes light up with excitement, and I vow right then that I’m going to give the girl presents every day of her life.

We both quickly dress. Once we’re done, I grab her hand and guide her over to the desk. I sit and then pull her into my lap. It’s amazing how easy this is for us. I suppose a couple of years of building desire will do that to two people.

I reach into my desk drawer and pull out a black velvet box. It’s small and holds something almost as pretty as she is. I lift the lid and hold it up for her. She plucks the ring from the holder and grins.

“This is gorgeous,” she breathes as she admires the blue stone that matches her eyes perfectly. “You shouldn’t have.”

I take her hand and then ease the ring on her finger. “I needed you to understand how much you mean to me, Jessie,” I tell her as I kiss her knuckle just above the ring. “I needed something you could look at every day. A promise to romance and love you until you’re ready for more.”

Her eyebrows lift and she smiles. “You plan to

romance me?"

"The plan was to romance you tomorrow night. The ring. A nice steak dinner. You and me. I've been waiting a long time for this. But then you had to go off and be naughty," I chide with a laugh. "Ruined all my plans." I wink at her and she swats at me.

"And to think I was off being bad, hoping my favorite cop would come arrest me. Dreams do come true," she teases.

I pull her to me and kiss her supple lips. "We still found our way together."

"Do you remember that time you stormed into my house, grabbed our neighbor Josh by his T-shirt, and then punched him right in the face?" she questions abruptly.

I wince because I'd been so enraged, I'd wanted to do much more than clock some teenage asshole in the nose. "I remember."

"Why'd you hit him? He refused to tell me." Her blue eyes are soft as she regards me.

I threatened him and told him if he told a soul, I'd arrest him. "I'd overhead him at Sonic, bragging to one of his buddies that he was going to 'hit that.'" My palm slides up under her dress and I let my longest finger graze along her pussy. Understanding dawns in her eyes. Her mouth parts in shock.

"Oh…"

"I followed him to your house and decked him because he most certainly was not allowed to hit," I growl as I stroke her clit, causing her to shudder, "that." I kiss her breast through her dress. "All of this was mine, even if I wasn't allowed to touch it yet."

She laughs. "Wow. Who knew you were such a brute? Just think, all this time I thought you saw me as an annoying kid."

"You were annoying, all right," I tease. "When you'd prance by wearing a pair of cutoff shorts with your ass hanging out whenever I'd be at your house having dinner, my cock would get embarrassingly hard, and *that* was annoying."

We're both chuckling when a deep voice booms from the doorway. I jerk my gaze over to see Sheriff McMahon glaring our way.

"I got a call from Gladys Morris on my cell that the station phone was down," he grumbles as he walks over to the cord, which is still unplugged, and proceeds to plug it back in. "It was down, all right. Can I ask what in the hell is going on here?"

Jessie slides off my lap and smooths out her dress. "I just came to visit Gentry for my birthday."

She flashes him a sweet smile. Her smiles disarm everyone. They always worked like a charm for me.

Sheriff scowls. "How old are you, anyway?"

She shrugs and challenges him with a gaze. "Not much younger than Mandy and perfectly legal."

He blanches at the mention of the town's bad girl. "Okay, you two," he grunts. "Just get out of here. I've got it from here."

I give him a quick nod of thanks and all but drag my girl out of the building. Once outside, I press her against the brick wall and kiss her until she's breathless. My cock is straining in my slacks once more. Apparently, it's making up for lost time.

"You're mine now, Jessie," I remind her again as I nip at her bottom lip.

She cups my cheeks and grins. "I always was."

The End

PLAYLIST

Listen on Spotify here.

"Obsession (Cover)" by Golden State
"Violet" by Hole
"I Will Possess Your Heart" by Death Cab for Cutie
"Tainted Love" by Marilyn Manson
"Even Though Our Love is Doomed" by Garbage
"(Don't Fear) The Reaper" by Blue Oyster Cult
"Afraid" by The Neighbourhood
"Black Sun" by Death Cab for Cutie
"Demons" by Imagine Dragons
"Motel" by Meg Myers
"Oh My" by Big Wreck
"Madness" by Muse
"Supermassive Black Hole" by Muse
"Wild Horses" by Bishop Briggs
"Way Down We Go" by Kaleo
"Uninvited" by Alanis Morissette
"River" by Bishop Briggs
"Are You Alone Now?" by Dead Sea Empire
"I Put A Spell On You" by Annie Lennox
"Life Like Mine" by Welles
"Deficiency" by Bad Pony
"Bringing Me Down (feat. Ruelle)" by Ki:Theory

BOOKS BY K WEBSTER

The Breaking the Rules Series:

Broken (Book 1)

Wrong (Book 2)

Scarred (Book 3)

Mistake (Book 4)

Crushed (Book 5 – a novella)

The Vegas Aces Series:

Rock Country (Book 1)

Rock Heart (Book 2)

Rock Bottom (Book 3)

The Becoming Her Series:

Becoming Lady Thomas (Book 1)

Becoming Countess Dumont (Book 2)

Becoming Mrs. Benedict (Book 3)

War & Peace Series:

This is War, Baby (Book 1)

This is Love, Baby (Book 2)

This Isn't Over, Baby (Book 3)

This Isn't You, Baby (Book 4)

This is Me, Baby (Book 5)

This Isn't Fair, Baby (Book 6)

This is the End, Baby (Book 7 – a novella)

2 Lovers Series:

Text 2 Lovers (Book 1)

Hate 2 Lovers (Book 2)

Alpha & Omega Duet:

Alpha & Omega (Book 1)

Omega & Love (Book 2)

Pretty Stolen Dolls Duet:

Pretty Stolen Dolls (Book 1)

Pretty Lost Dolls (Book 2)

Taboo Treats (Standalones):

Bad Bad Bad

Easton

Standalone Novels:

Apartment 2B

Love and Law

Moth to a Flame

Erased

The Road Back to Us

Surviving Harley

Give Me Yesterday

Running Free

Dirty Ugly Toy

Zeke's Eden

Sweet Jayne

Untimely You

Mad Sea

Whispers and the Roars

Schooled by a Senior

B-Sides and Rarities

Blue Hill Blood by Elizabeth Gray

Notice

ACKNOWLEDGEMENTS

Thank you to my husband…I love you, honey!

A huge thank you to my Krazy for K Webster's Books reader group. You all are insanely supportive and I can't thank you enough. Your love for taboo feeds my desire to write it.

A gigantic thank you to my betas who read this story. Elizabeth Clinton, Ella Stewart, and Misty Walker, you all helped make this story even better. Your feedback and early reading is important to this entire process and I can't thank you enough.

A big thank you to my author friends who have given me your friendship and your support. You have no idea how much that means to me.

Thank you to all of my blogger friends both big and small that go above and beyond to always share my stuff. You all rock! #AllBlogsMatter

Ellie at Love N Books, thank you for editing my preacher man! You were quick and your turnaround was awesome. You're the best!

Vanessa with Prema Editing, thank you for editing Deputy Adair. You're amazing!

Thank you Stacey Blake for being a super star as always when formatting my books and in general. I love you! I love you! I love you!

A big thanks to my PR gal, Nicole Blanchard. You are fabulous at what you do and keep me on track!

Lastly but certainly not least of all, thank you to all of the wonderful readers out there that are willing to hear my story and enjoy my characters like I do. It means the world to me!

ABOUT THE AUTHOR

K Webster is the author of dozens of romance books in many different genres including contemporary romance, historical romance, paranormal romance, taboo romance, dark romance, romantic suspense, and erotic romance. When not spending time with her hilarious and handsome husband and two adorable children, she's active on social media connecting with her readers.

Her other passions besides writing include reading and graphic design. K can always be found in front of her computer chasing her next idea and taking action. She looks forward to the day when she will see one of her titles on the big screen.

Join K Webster's newsletter to receive a couple of updates a month on new releases and exclusive content. To join, all you need to do is go here.

www.authorkwebster.us10.list-manage.com/
subscribe?u=36473e274a1bf9597b508ea72&id=96366bb08e

Facebook: www.facebook.com/authorkwebster

Blog: authorkwebster.wordpress.com

Twitter: @KristiWebster

Email: kristi@authorkwebster.com

Goodreads:
www.goodreads.com/user/show/10439773-k-webster

Instagram: instagram.com/kristiwebster